BRIDGE TO
TERABITHIA

Katherine Paterson

BRIDGE TO TERABITHIA

Illustrated by Donna Diamond

AN AVON CAMELOT BOOK

*The Song "Free To Be... You and Me" by Stephen
Lawrence and Bruce Hart. Copyright © 1972.
Ms. Foundation for Women, Inc. Used by permission.*

AVON BOOKS
A division of
The Hearst Corporation
1790 Broadway
New York, New York 10019

Copyright © 1977 by Katherine Paterson
Published by arrangement with Harper and Row Publishers, Inc.
Library of Congress Catalog Card Number: 78-70995
ISBN: 0-380-43281-1

First Camelot Printing, September, 1978

AVON TRADEMARK REG. U.S. PAT. OFF. AND IN
OTHER COUNTRIES. MARCA REGISTRADA, HECHO EN
U.S.A.

Printed in the U.S.A.

DON   20   19   18   17

KATHERINE PATERSON is the author of THE MASTER PUPPETEER, which won the 1977 National Book Award, and THE GREAT GILLY HOPKINS, as well as many more books for young readers. Several of her novels have been chosen as Notable Children's Books by the American Library Association. Ms. Paterson was born in China and spent part of her childhood there. She also lived, studied and taught in Japan. Her four children and their friends have provided her with some of the subject matter for her sharply observant stories of family life. She lives with her husband and children in Takoma Park, Maryland.

DONNA DIAMOND is a graduate of the High School of Music and Art in New York City, and received her Bachelor of Fine Arts from Boston University. She began illustrating four years ago, and has since illustrated seven books for young readers. BRIDGE TO TERABITHIA was illustrated almost entirely to music by the Beatles. Ms. Diamond lives in New York City.

I wrote this book
for my son
David Lord Paterson,
but after he read it
he asked me to put Lisa's name
on this page as well,
and so I do.
For
David Paterson and Lisa Hill,
banzai

Contents

BRIDGE TO TERABITHIA

Jesse Oliver Aarons, Jr.

Ba-room, ba-room, ba-room, baripity, baripity, baripity, baripity—Good. His dad had the pickup going. He could get up now. Jess slid out of bed and into his overalls. He didn't worry about a shirt because once he began running he would be hot as popping grease even if the morning air was chill, or shoes because the bottoms of his feet were by now as tough as his worn-out sneakers.

"Where you going, Jess?" May Belle lifted herself up sleepily from the double bed where she and Joyce Ann slept.

"*Sh.*" He warned. The walls were thin. Momma would be mad as flies in a fruit jar if they woke her up this time of day.

He patted May Belle's hair and yanked the twisted sheet up to her small chin. "Just over the cow field," he whispered. May Belle smiled and snuggled down under the sheet.

"Gonna run?"

"Maybe."

Of course he was going to run. He had gotten up early every day all summer to run. He figured if he worked at it—and Lord, had he worked—he could be the fastest runner in the fifth grade when school opened up. He had to be the fastest—not one of the fastest or next to the fastest, but *the* fastest. The very best.

He tiptoed out of the house. The place was so rattly that it screeched whenever you put your foot down, but Jess had found that if you tiptoed, it gave only a low moan, and he could usually get outdoors without waking Momma or Ellie or Brenda or Joyce Ann. May Belle was another matter. She was going on seven, and she worshiped him, which was OK sometimes. When you were the only boy smashed between four sisters, and the older two had despised you ever since you stopped letting them dress you up and wheel you around in their rusty old doll carriage, and the littlest one cried if you looked at her cross-eyed, it was nice to have somebody who worshiped you. Even if it got unhandy sometimes.

He began to trot across the yard. His breath was coming out in little puffs—cold for August. But it was early yet. By noontime when his mom would have him out working, it would be hot enough.

Miss Bessie stared at him sleepily as he climbed across the scrap heap, over the fence, and into the cow field. "*Moo—oo*," she said, looking for all the world like another May Belle with her big, brown droopy eyes.

"Hey, Miss Bessie," Jess said soothingly. "Just go on back to sleep."

Miss Bessie strolled over to a greenish patch—most of the field was brown and dry—and yanked up a mouthful.

"That'a girl. Just eat your breakfast. Don't pay me no mind."

He always started at the northwest corner of the field, crouched over like the runners he had seen on *Wide World of Sports*.

"Bang," he said, and took off flying around the cow field. Miss Bessie strolled toward the center, still following him with her droopy eyes, chewing slowly. She didn't look very smart, even for a cow, but she was plenty bright enough to get out of Jess's way.

His straw-colored hair flapped hard against his forehead, and his arms and legs flew out every which way. He had never learned to run properly, but he was long-legged for a ten-year-old, and no one had more grit than he.

Lark Creek Elementary was short on everything, especially athletic equipment, so all the balls went to the upper grades at recess time after lunch. Even if a fifth grader started out the period with a ball, it was sure to be in the hands of a sixth or seventh grader before the hour was half over. The older boys always took the dry center of the upper field for their ball games, while the girls claimed the small top section for hopscotch and jump rope and hanging around talking. So the lower-grade boys had started this running thing. They would all line up on the far side of the lower field, where it was either muddy or deep crusty ruts. Earle Watson who was no good at running, but had a big mouth, would yell "Bang!" and they'd race to a line they'd toed across at the other end.

One time last year Jesse had won. Not just the first heat but the whole shebang. Only once. But it had put into his mouth a taste for winning. Ever since he'd been in first grade he'd been that "crazy little kid that draws all the time." But one day—April the twenty-second, a drizzly Monday, it had been—he ran ahead of them all, the red mud slooching up through the holes in the bottom of his sneakers.

For the rest of that day, and until after lunch on the next, he had been "the fastest kid in the third, fourth, *and* fifth grades," and he only a fourth grader. On Tuesday, Wayne Pettis had won again as usual. But this year Wayne Pettis would be in the sixth grade. He'd play football until Christmas and baseball until June with the rest of the big guys. Anybody had a chance to be the fastest runner, and by Miss Bessie, this year it was going to be Jesse Oliver Aarons, Jr.

Jess pumped his arms harder and bent his head for the distant fence. He could hear the third-grade boys screaming him on. They would follow him around like a country-music star. And May Belle would pop her buttons. *Her brother* was the fastest, the best. That ought to give the rest of the first grade something to chew their cuds on.

Even his dad would be proud. Jess rounded the corner. He couldn't keep going quite so fast, but he continued running for a while—it would build him up. May Belle would tell Daddy, so it wouldn't look as though he, Jess, was a bragger.

Maybe Dad would be so proud he'd forget all about how tired he was from the long drive back and forth to Washington and the digging and hauling all day. He would get right down on the floor and wrestle, the way they used to. Old Dad would be surprised at how strong he'd gotten in the last couple of years.

His body was begging him to quit, but Jess pushed it on. He had to let that puny chest of his know who was boss.

"Jess." It was May Belle yelling from the other side of the scrap heap. "Momma says you gotta come in and eat now. Leave the milking til later."

Oh, crud. He'd run too long. Now everyone would know he'd been out and start in on him.

"Yeah, OK." He turned, still running, and headed for the scrap heap. Without breaking his rhythm, he climbed over the fence, scrambled across the scrap heap, thumped May Belle on the head ("Owww!"), and trotted on to the house.

"We-ell, look at the big O-lympic star," said Ellie, banging two cups onto the table, so that the strong, black coffee sloshed out. "Sweating like a knock-kneed mule."

Jess pushed his damp hair out of his face and plunked down on the wooden bench. He dumped two spoonfuls of sugar into his cup and slurped to keep the hot coffee from scalding his mouth.

"*Oooo*, Momma, he stinks." Brenda pinched her nose with her pinky crooked delicately. "Make him wash."

"Get over here to the sink and wash yourself," his mother said without raising her eyes from the stove. "And step on it. These grits are scorching the bottom of the pot already."

"Momma! Not again," Brenda whined.

Lord, he was tired. There wasn't a muscle in his body that didn't ache.

"You heard what Momma said," Ellie yelled at his back.

"I can't stand it, Momma!" Brenda again. "Make him get his smelly self off this bench."

Jess put his cheek down on the bare wood of the tabletop.

"Jess-*see!*" His mother was looking now. "And put on a shirt."

"Yes'm." He dragged himself to the sink. The water he flipped on his face and up his arms pricked like ice. His hot skin crawled under the cold drops.

May Belle was standing in the kitchen door watching him. "Get me a shirt, May Belle."

She looked as if her mouth was set to say no, but instead she said, "You shouldn't ought to beat me in the head," and went off obediently to fetch his T-shirt. Good old May Belle. Joyce Ann would have been screaming yet from that little tap. Four-year-olds were a pure pain.

"I got plenty of chores needs doing around here this morning," his mother announced as they were finishing the grits and red gravy. His mother was from Georgia and still cooked like it.

"Oh, *Momma!*" Ellie and Brenda squawked in concert. Those girls could get out of work faster than grasshoppers could slip through your fingers.

"Momma, you promised me and Brenda we could go to Millsburg for school shopping."

"You ain't got no money for school shopping!"

"*Momma.* We're just going to look around." Lord, he wished Brenda would stop whining so. "*Christmas!* You don't want us to have no fun at all."

"*Any* fun," Ellie corrected her primly.

"Oh, shuttup."

Ellie ignored her. "Miz Timmons is coming by to pick us up. I told Lollie Sunday you said it was OK. I feel dumb calling her and saying you changed your mind."

"Oh, all right. But I ain't got no money to give you."

Any money, something whispered inside Jess's head.

"I know, Momma. We'll just take the five dollars Daddy promised us. No more'n that."

"What five dollars?"

"Oh, Momma, you *remember*." Ellie's voice was sweeter than a melted Mars Bar. "Daddy said last week we girls were going to have to have *something* for school."

"Oh, take it," his mother said angrily, reaching for her cracked vinyl purse on the shelf above the stove. She counted out five wrinkled bills.

"Momma"—Brenda was starting again—"can't we have just one more? So it'll be three each?"

"No!"

"Momma, you can't buy nothing for two fifty. Just one little pack of notebook paper's gone up to . . ."

"No!"

Ellie got up noisily and began to clear the table. "Your turn to wash, Brenda," she said loudly.

"*Awww*, Ellie."

Ellie jabbed her with a spoon. Jesse saw that look. Brenda shut up her whine halfway out of her Rose Lustre lipsticked mouth. She wasn't as smart as Ellie, but even she knew not to push Momma too far.

Which left Jess to do the work as usual. Momma never sent the babies out to help, although if he worked it right he could usually get May Belle to do something. He put his head down on the table. The running had done him in this morning. Through his top ear came the sound of the Timmonses' old Buick—"Wants oil," his dad would say—and the happy buzz of voices outside the screen door as Ellie and Brenda squashed in among the seven Timmonses.

"All right, Jesse. Get your lazy self off that bench. Miss

Bessie's bag is probably dragging ground by now. And you still got beans to pick."

Lazy. *He* was the lazy one. He gave his poor deadweight of a head one minute more on the tabletop.

"Jess-*see!*"

"OK, Momma. I'm *going.*"

It was May Belle who came to tell him in the bean patch that people were moving into the old Perkins place down on the next farm. Jess wiped his hair out of his eyes and squinted. Sure enough. A U-Haul was parked right by the door. One of those big jointed ones. These people had a lot of junk. But they wouldn't last. The Perkins place was one of those ratty old country houses you moved into because you had no decent place to go and moved out of as quickly as you could. He thought later how peculiar it was that here was probably the biggest thing in his life, and he had shrugged it off as nothing.

The flies were buzzing around his sweating face and shoulders. He dropped the beans into the bucket and swatted with both hands. "Get me my shirt, May Belle." The flies were more important than any U-Haul.

May Belle jogged to the end of the row and picked up his T-shirt from where it had been discarded earlier. She walked back holding it with two fingers way out in front of her. "*Oooo,* it stinks," she said, just as Brenda would have.

"Shuttup," he said and grabbed the shirt away from her.

Leslie Burke

Ellie and Brenda weren't back by seven. Jess had finished all the picking and helped his mother can the beans. She never canned except when it was scalding hot anyhow, and all the boiling turned the kitchen into some kind of hellhole. Of course, her temper had been terrible, and she had screamed at Jess all afternoon and was now too tired to fix any supper.

Jess made peanut-butter sandwiches for the little girls and himself, and because the kitchen was still hot and almost nauseatingly full of bean smell, the three of them went outside to eat.

The U-Haul was still out by the Perkins place. He couldn't see anybody moving outside, so they must have finished unloading.

"I hope they have a girl, six or seven," said May Belle. "I need somebody to play with."

"You got Joyce Ann."

"I hate Joyce Ann. She's nothing but a baby."

Joyce Ann's lip went out. They both watched it tremble. Then her pudgy body shuddered, and she let out a great cry.

"Who's teasing the baby?" his mother yelled out the screen door.

Jess sighed and poked the last of his sandwich into Joyce Ann's open mouth. Her eyes went wide, and she clamped her jaws down on the unexpected gift. Now maybe he could have some peace.

He closed the screen door gently as he entered and slipped past his mother, who was rocking herself in the kitchen chair watching TV. In the room he shared with the little ones, he dug under his mattress and pulled out his pad and pencils. Then, stomach down on the bed, he began to draw.

Jess drew the way some people drink whiskey. The peace would start at the top of his muddled brain and seep down through his tired and tensed-up body. Lord, he loved to draw. Animals, mostly. Not regular animals like Miss Bessie or the chickens, but crazy animals with problems—for some reason he liked to put his beasts into impossible fixes. This one was a hippopotamus just leaving the edge of the cliff, turning over and over—you could tell by the curving lines—in the air toward the sea below where surprised fish were leaping goggle-eyed out of the water. There was a balloon over the hippopotamus—where his head should have been but his bottom actually was—"Oh!" it was saying. "I seem to have forgot my glasses."

Jesse began to smile. If he decided to show it to May Belle, he would have to explain the joke, but once he did, she would laugh like a live audience on TV.

He would like to show his drawings to his dad, but he didn't dare. When he was in first grade, he had told his dad that he

wanted to be an artist when he grew up. He'd thought his dad would be pleased. He wasn't. "What are they teaching in that damn school?" he had asked. "Bunch of old ladies turning my only son into some kind of a—" He had stopped on the word, but Jess had gotten the message. It was one you didn't forget, even after four years.

The devil of it was that none of his regular teachers ever liked his drawings. When they'd catch him scribbling, they'd screech about waste—wasted time, wasted paper, wasted ability. Except Miss Edmunds, the music teacher. She was the only one he dared show anything to, and she'd only been at school one year, and then only on Fridays.

Miss Edmunds was one of his secrets. He was in love with her. Not the kind of silly stuff Ellie and Brenda giggled about on the telephone. This was too real and too deep to talk about, even to think about very much. Her long swishy black hair and blue, blue eyes. She could play the guitar like a regular recording star, and she had this soft floaty voice that made Jess squish inside. Lord, she was gorgeous. And she liked him, too.

One day last winter he had given her one of his pictures. Just shoved it into her hand after class and run. The next Friday she had asked him to stay a minute after class. She said he was "unusually talented," and she hoped he wouldn't let anything discourage him, but would "keep it up." That meant, Jess believed, that she thought he was the best. It was not the kind of best that counted either at school or at home, but it was a genuine kind of best. He kept the knowledge of it buried inside himself like a pirate treasure. He was rich, very rich, but no one could know about it for now except his fellow outlaw, Julia Edmunds.

"Sounds like some kinda hippie," his mother had said

when Brenda, who had been in seventh grade last year, described Miss Edmunds to her.

She probably was. Jess wouldn't argue that, but he saw her as a beautiful wild creature who had been caught for a moment in that dirty old cage of a schoolhouse, perhaps by mistake. But he hoped, he prayed, she'd never get loose and fly away. He managed to endure the whole boring week of school for that one half hour on Friday afternoons when they'd sit on the worn-out rug on the floor of the teachers' room (there was no place else in the building for Miss Edmunds to spread out all her stuff) and sing songs like "My Beautiful Balloon," "This Land Is Your Land," "Free to Be You and Me," "Blowing in the Wind," and because Mr. Turner, the principal, insisted, "God Bless America."

Miss Edmunds would play her guitar and let the kids take turns on the autoharp, the triangles, cymbals, tambourines, and bongo drum. Lord, could they ever make a racket! All the teachers hated Fridays. And a lot of the kids pretended to.

But Jess knew what fakes they were. Sniffing "hippie" and "peacenik," even though the Vietnam War was over and it was supposed to be OK again to like peace, the kids would make fun of Miss Edmunds' lack of lipstick or the cut of her jeans. She was, of course, the only female teacher anyone had ever seen in Lark Creek Elementary wearing pants. In Washington and its fancy suburbs, even in Millsburg, that was OK, but Lark Creek was the backwash of fashion. It took them a long time to accept there what everyone could see by their TV's was OK anywhere else.

So the students of Lark Creek Elementary sat at their desks all Friday, their hearts thumping with anticipation as they listened to the joyful pandemonium pouring out from the teachers' room, spent their allotted half hours with Miss Edmunds under the spell of her wild beauty and in the snare of her enthusiasms, and then went out and pretended that they couldn't be suckered by some hippie in tight jeans with make-up all over her eyes but none on her mouth.

Jess just kept his mouth shut. It wouldn't help to try to defend Miss Edmunds against their unjust and hypocritical attacks. Besides, she was beyond such stupid behavior. It couldn't touch her. But whenever possible, he stole a few minutes on Friday just to stand close to her and hear her voice, soft and smooth as suede, assuring him that he was a "neat kid."

We're alike, Jess would tell himself, me and Miss Edmunds. Beautiful Julia. The syllables rolled through his head like a ripple of guitar chords. We don't belong at Lark Creek, Julia and me. "You're the proverbial diamond in the rough," she'd said to him once, touching his nose lightly with the tip of her electrifying finger. But it was she who was the diamond, sparkling out of that muddy, grassless, dirty-brick setting.

"Jess-*see*!"

Jess shoved the pad and pencils under his mattress and lay down flat, his heart thumping against the quilt.

His mother was at the door. "You milk yet?"

He jumped off the bed. "Just going to." He dodged around her and out, grabbing the pail from beside the sink and the stool from beside the door, before she could ask him what he had been up to.

Lights were winking out from all three floors of the old Perkins place. It was nearly dark. Miss Bessie's bag was tight, and she was fidgeting with discomfort. She should have been milked a couple of hours ago. He eased himself onto the stool and began to tug; the warm milk pinged into the pail. Down on the road an occasional truck passed by with its dimmers on.

His dad would be home soon, and so would those cagey girls who managed somehow to have all the fun and leave him and their mother with all the work. He wondered what they had bought with all their money. Lord, what he wouldn't give for a new pad of real art paper and a set of those marking pens—color pouring out onto the page as fast as you could think it. Not like stubby school crayons you had to press down on till somebody bitched about your breaking them.

A car was turning in. It was the Timmonses'. The girls had beat Dad home. Jess could hear their happy calls as the car doors slammed. Momma would fix them supper, and when he went in with the milk, he'd find them all laughing and chattering. Momma'd even forget she was tired and mad. He was the only one who had to take that stuff. Sometimes he felt so lonely among all these females—even the one rooster had died, and they hadn't yet gotten another. With his father gone from sunup until well past dark, who was there to know how he felt? Weekends weren't any better. His dad was so tired from the wear and tear of the week and trying to catch up around the place that when he wasn't actually working, he was sleeping in front of the TV.

"Hey, Jesse." May Belle. The dumb kid wouldn't even let you think privately.

"What do you want now?"

He watched her shrink two sizes. "I got something to tell you." She hung her head.

"You ought to be in bed," he said huffily, mad at himself for cutting her down.

"Ellie and Brenda come home."

"Came. Came home." Why couldn't he quit picking on her?

But her news was too delicious to let him stop her sharing it. "Ellie bought herself a see-through blouse, and Momma's throwing a fit!"

Good, he thought. "That ain't nothing to cheer about," he said.

Baripity, baripity, baripity.

"Daddy!" May Belle screamed with delight and started running for the road. Jess watched his dad stop the truck, lean over to unlatch the door, so May Belle could climb in. He turned away. Durn lucky kid. She could run after him and grab him and kiss him. It made Jess ache inside to watch his dad grab the little ones to his shoulder, or lean down and hug them. It seemed to him that he had been thought too big for that since the day he was born.

When the pail was full, he gave Miss Bessie a pat to move her away. Putting the stool under his left arm, he carried the heavy pail carefully, so none of the milk would slop out.

"Mighty late with the milking, aren't you, son?" It was the only thing his father said directly to him all evening.

The next morning he almost didn't get up at the sound of the pickup. He could feel, even before he came fully awake, how tired he still was. But May Belle was grinning at him, propped up on one elbow. "Ain't 'cha gonna run?" she asked.

"No," he said, shoving the sheet away. "I'm gonna fly."

Because he was more tired than usual, he had to push himself harder. He pretended that Wayne Pettis was there, just ahead of him, and he had to keep up. His feet pounded the uneven ground, and he thrashed his arms harder and harder. He'd catch him. "Watch out, Wayne Pettis," he said between his teeth. "I'll get you. You can't beat me."

"If you're so afraid of the cow," the voice said, "why don't you just climb the fence?"

He paused in midair like a stop-action TV shot and turned,

almost losing his balance, to face the questioner, who was sitting on the fence nearest the old Perkins place, dangling bare brown legs. The person had jaggedy brown hair cut close to its face and wore one of those blue undershirtlike tops with faded jeans cut off above the knees. He couldn't honestly tell whether it was a girl or a boy.

"Hi," he or she said, jerking his or her head toward the Perkins place. "We just moved in."

Jess stood where he was, staring.

The person slid off the fence and came toward him. "I thought we might as well be friends," it said. "There's no one else close by."

Girl, he decided. Definitely a girl, but he couldn't have said why he was suddenly sure. She was about his height—not quite though, he was pleased to realize as she came nearer.

"My name's Leslie Burke."

She even had one of those dumb names that could go either way, but he was sure now that he was right.

"What's the matter?"

"Huh?"

"Is something the matter?"

"Yeah. No." He pointed his thumb in the direction of his own house, and then wiped his hair off his forehead. "Jess Aarons." Too bad May Belle's girl came in the wrong size. "Well—well." He nodded at her. "See you." He turned toward the house. No use trying to run any more this morning. Might as well milk Miss Bessie and get that out of the way.

"Hey!" Leslie was standing in the middle of the cow field, her head tilted and her hands on her hips. "Where you going?"

"I got work to do," he called back over his shoulder. When he came out later with the pail and stool, she was gone.

The Fastest Kid in the Fifth Grade

Jess didn't see Leslie Burke again except from a distance until the first day of school, the following Tuesday, when Mr. Turner brought her down to Mrs. Myers' fifth-grade class at Lark Creek Elementary.

Leslie was still dressed in the faded cutoffs and the blue undershirt. She had sneakers on her feet but no socks. Surprise swooshed up from the class like steam from a released radiator cap. They were all sitting there primly dressed in their spring Sunday best. Even Jess wore his one pair of corduroys and an ironed shirt.

The reaction didn't seem to bother her. She stood there in front, her eyes saying, "OK, friends, here I am," in answer to their open-mouthed stares while Mrs. Myers fluttered about trying to figure where to put the extra desk. The room was a small basement one, and five rows of six desks already filled it more than comfortably.

"Thirty-one," Mrs. Myers kept mumbling over her double

chin, "thirty-one. No one else has more than twenty-nine." She finally decided to put the desk up against the side wall near the front. "Just there for now—uh—Leslie. It's the best we can do—for now. This is a very crowded classroom." She swung a pointed glance at Mr. Turner's retreating form.

Leslie waited quietly until the seventh-grade boy who'd been sent down with the extra desk scraped it into position hard against the radiator and under the first window. Without making any noise, she pulled it a few inches forward from the radiator and settled herself into it. Then she turned once more to gaze at the rest of the class.

Thirty pairs of eyes were suddenly focused on desk-top scratches. Jess ran his forefinger around the heart with two pairs of initials, BR + SK, trying to figure out whose desk he had inherited. Probably Sally Koch's. Girls did more of the heart stuff in fifth grade than boys. Besides BR must be Billy Rudd, and Billy was known to favor Myrna Hauser last spring. Of course, these initials might have been here longer than that, in which case . . .

"Jesse Aarons. Bobby Greggs. Pass out the arithmetic books. Please." On the last word, Mrs. Myers flashed her famous first-day-of-school smile. It was said in the upper grades that Mrs. Myers had never been seen to smile except on the first and the last day of school.

Jess roused himself and went to the front. As he passed Leslie's desk, she grinned and rippled her fingers low in a kind of wave. He jerked a nod. He couldn't help feeling sorry for her. It must be embarrassing to sit in front when you find yourself dressed funny on the first day of school. And you don't know anybody.

He slapped the books down as Mrs. Myers directed. Gary Fulcher grabbed his arm as he went by. "Gonna run today?"

Jess nodded. Gary smirked. *He thinks he can beat me, the dumbhead.* At the thought, something jiggled inside Jess. He knew he was better than he had been last spring. Fulcher might think he was going to be the best, now that Wayne Pettis was in sixth, but he, Jess, planned to give old Fulcher a *le-etle* surprise come noon. It was as though he had swallowed grasshoppers. He could hardly wait.

Mrs. Myers handed out books almost as though she were President of the United States, dragging the distribution process out in senseless signings and ceremonies. It occcurred to Jess that she, too, wished to postpone regular school as long as possible. When it wasn't his turn to pass out books, Jess sneaked out a piece of notebook paper and drew. He was toying with the idea of doing a whole book of drawings. He ought to choose one chief character and do a story about it. He scribbled several animals and tried to think of a name. A good title would get him started. *The Haunted Hippo*? He liked the ring of it. *Herby the Haunted Hippo*? Even better. *The Case of the Crooked Crocodile*. Not bad.

"Whatcha drawing?" Gary Fulcher was leaning way over his desk.

Jess covered the page with his arm. "Nothing."

"Ah, c'mon. Lemme see."

Jess shook his head.

Gary reached down and tried to pull Jess's hand away from the paper. "The Case of the Crooked—c'mon, Jess," he whispered hoarsely. "I ain't gonna hurt nothing." He yanked at Jess's thumb.

Jess put both arms over the paper and brought his sneaker heel crashing down on Gary Fulcher's toe.

"*Ye-ow!*"

"Boys!" Mrs. Myers' face had lost its lemon-pie smile.

"He stomped my toe."

"Take your seat, Gary."

"But he—"

"Sit down!"

"Jesse Aarons. One more peep from your direction and you can spend recess in here. Copying the dictionary."

Jess's face was burning hot. He slid the notebook paper back under his desk top and put his head down. A whole year of this. Eight more years of this. He wasn't sure he could stand it.

🍃

The children ate lunch at their desks. The county had been promising Lark Creek a lunchroom for twenty years, but there never seemed to be enough money. Jess had been so careful not to lose his recess time that even now he chewed his bologna sandwich with his lips tight shut and his eyes on the initialed heart. Around him conversations buzzed. They were not supposed to talk during lunch, but it was the first day and even Monster-Mouth Myers shot fewer flames on the first day.

"She's eating clabber." Two seats up from where he sat, Mary Lou Peoples was at work being the second snottiest girl in the fifth grade.

"Yogurt, stupid. Don't you watch TV?" This from Wanda Kay Moore, the snottiest, who sat immediately in front of Jess.

"Yuk."

Lord, why couldn't they leave people in peace? Why shouldn't Leslie Burke eat anything she durn pleased?

He forgot that he was trying to eat carefully and took a loud slurp of his milk.

Wanda Moore turned around, all priss-face. "Jesse Aarons. That noise is pure repulsive."

He glared at her hard and gave another slurp.

"You are disgusting."

Brrrrring. The recess bell. With a yelp, the boys were pushing for first place at the door.

"The boys will all sit down." Oh, Lord. "While the girls line up to go out to the playground. Ladies first."

The boys quivered on the edges of their seats like moths fighting to be freed of cocoons. Would she never let them go?

"All right, now if you boys . . ." They didn't give her a chance to change her mind. They were halfway to the end of the field before she could finish her sentence.

The first two out began dragging their toes to make the finish line. The ground was rutted from past rains, but had hardened in the late summer drought, so they had to give up on sneaker toes and draw the line with a stick. The fifth-grade boys, bursting with new importance, ordered the fourth graders this way and that, while the smaller boys tried to include themselves without being conspicuous.

"How many you guys gonna run?" Gary Fulcher demanded.

"Me—me—me." Everyone yelled.

"That's too many. No first, second, *or* third graders—except maybe the Butcher cousins and Timmy Vaughn. The rest of you will just be in the way."

Shoulders sagged, but the little boys backed away obediently.

"OK. That leaves twenty-six, twenty-seven—stand still—twenty-eight. You get twenty-eight, Greg?" Fulcher asked Greg Williams, his shadow.

"Right. Twenty-eight."

"OK. Now. We'll have eliminations like always. Count off by fours. Then we'll run all the ones together, then the twos—"

"We know. We know." Everyone was impatient with Gary, who was trying for all the world to sound like this year's Wayne Pettis.

Jess was a four, which suited him well enough. He was impatient to run, but he really didn't mind having a chance to see how the others were doing since spring. Fulcher was a one, of course, having started everything with himself. Jess grinned at Fulcher's back and stuck his hands into the pockets of his corduroys, wriggling his right forefinger through the hole.

Gary won the first heat easily and had plenty of breath left to boss the organizing of the second. A few of the younger boys drifted off to play King of the Mountain on the slope between the upper and lower fields. Out of the corner of his eye, Jess saw someone coming down from the upper field. He turned his back and pretended to concentrate on Fulcher's high-pitched commands.

"Hi." Leslie Burke had come up beside him.

He shifted slightly away. "Umph."

"Aren't you running?"

"Later." Maybe if he didn't look at her, she would go back to the upper field where she belonged.

Gary told Earle Watson to bang the start. Jess watched. Nobody with much speed in that crowd. He kept his eyes on the shirttails and bent backs.

A fight broke out at the finish line between Jimmy Mitchell and Clyde Deal. Everyone rushed to see. Jess was aware that Leslie Burke stayed at his elbow, but he was careful not to look her way.

"Clyde." Gary Fulcher made his declaration. "It was Clyde."

"It was a tie, Fulcher," a fourth grader protested. "I was standing right here."

"Clyde Deal."

Jimmy Mitchell's jaw was set. "I won, Fulcher. You couldn't even see from way back there."

"It was Deal." Gary ignored the protests. "We're wasting time. All threes line up. Right now."

Jimmy's fists went up. "Ain't fair, Fulcher."

Gary turned his back and headed for the starting line.

"Oh, let 'em both run in the finals. What's it gonna hurt?" Jess said loudly.

Gary stopped walking and wheeled to face him. Fulcher glared first at Jess and then at Leslie Burke. "Next thing," he said, his voice dripping with sarcasm, "next thing you're gonna want to let some *girl* run."

Jess's face went hot. "Sure," he said recklessly. "Why not?" He turned deliberately toward Leslie. "Wanna run?" he asked.

"Sure." She was grinning. "Why not?"

"You ain't scared to let a girl race are you, Fulcher?"

For a minute he thought Gary was going to sock him, and he stiffened. He mustn't let Fulcher suspect that he was scared of a little belt in the mouth. But instead Gary broke into a trot and started bossing the threes into line for their heat.

"You can run with the fours, Leslie." He said it loudly enough to make sure Fulcher could hear him and then concentrated on the runners. See, he told himself, you can stand up to a creep like Fulcher. No sweat.

Bobby Miller won the threes easily. He was the best of the fourth graders, almost as fast as Fulcher. *But not as good as me*, Jess thought. He was beginning to get really excited now. There wasn't anybody in the fours who could give him much of a race. Still it would be better to give Fulcher a scare by running well in the heat.

Leslie lined up beside him on the right. He moved a tiny bit to the left, but she didn't seem to notice.

At the bang Jess shot forward. It felt good—even the rough ground against the bottom of his worn sneakers. He was pumping good. He could almost smell Gary Fulcher's surprise at his improvement. The crowd was noisier than they'd been during the other heats. Maybe they were all noticing. He wanted to look back and see where the others were, but he resisted the temptation. It would seem conceited to look back. He concentrated on the line ahead. It was nearing with every step. "Oh, Miss Bessie, if you could see me now."

He felt it before he saw it. Someone was moving up. He automatically pumped harder. Then the shape was there in his sideways vision. Then suddenly pulling ahead. He forced himself now. His breath was choking him, and the sweat was in his eyes. But he saw the figure anyhow. The faded cutoffs crossed the line a full three feet ahead of him.

Leslie turned to face him with a wide smile on her tanned face. He stumbled and without a word began half walking, half trotting over to the starting line. This was the day he was going to be champion—the best runner of the fourth and fifth grades, and he hadn't even won his heat. There was no cheering at either end of the field. The rest of the boys seemed as stunned as he. The teasing would come later, he felt sure, but at least for the moment none of them were talking.

"OK." Fulcher took over. He tried to appear very much in charge. "OK, you guys. You can line up for the finals." He walked over to Leslie. "OK, you had your fun. You can run on up to the hopscotch now."

"But I won the heat," she said.

Gary lowered his head like a bull. "Girls aren't supposed to play on the lower field. Better get up there before one of the teachers sees you."

"I want to run," she said quietly.

"You already did."

"Whatsa matter, Fulcher?" All Jess's anger was bubbling out. He couldn't seem to stop the flow. "Whatsa matter? Scared to race her?"

Fulcher's fist went up. But Jess walked away from it. Fulcher would have to let her run now, he knew. And Fulcher did, angrily and grudgingly.

She beat him. She came in first and turned her large shining eyes on a bunch of dumb sweating-mad faces. The bell rang. Jess started across the lower field, his hands still deep in his pockets. She caught up with him. He took his hands out and began to trot toward the hill. She'd got him into enough trouble. She speeded up and refused to be shaken off.

"Thanks," she said.

"Yeah?" For what? he was thinking.

"You're the only kid in this whole durned school who's worth shooting." He wasn't sure, he thought her voice was quivering, but he wasn't going to start feeling sorry for her again.

"So shoot me," he said.

On the bus that afternoon he did something he had never thought he would do. He sat down beside May Belle. It was the only way he could make sure that he wouldn't have Leslie plunking herself down beside him. Lord, the girl had no notion of what you did and didn't do. He stared out the window, but he knew she had come and was sitting across the aisle from them.

He heard her say "Jess" once, but the bus was noisy enough that he could pretend he hadn't heard. When they came to the stop, he grabbed May Belle's hand and dragged her off, conscious that Leslie was right behind them. But she didn't try to speak to him again, nor did she follow them. She just took off running to the old Perkins place. He couldn't help turning to watch. She ran as though it was her nature. It reminded him of the flight of wild ducks in the autumn. So smooth. The word "beautiful" came to his mind, but he shook it away and hurried up toward the house.

Rulers of
Terabithia

Because school had started on the first Tuesday after Labor Day, it was a short week. It was a good thing because each day was worse than the one before. Leslie continued to join the boys at recess, and every day she won. By Friday a number of the fourth- and fifth-grade boys had already drifted away to play King of the Mountain on the slope between the two fields. Since there were only a handful left, they didn't even have to have heats, which took away a lot of the suspense. Running wasn't fun anymore. And it was all Leslie's fault.

Jess knew now that he would never be the best runner of the fourth and fifth grades, and his only consolation was that neither would Gary Fulcher. They went through the motions of the contest on Friday, but when it was over and Leslie had won again, everyone sort of knew without saying so that it was the end of the races.

At least it was Friday, and Miss Edmunds was back. The

fifth grade had music right after recess. Jess had passed Miss Edmunds in the hall earlier in the day, and she had stopped him and made a fuss over him. "Did you keep drawing this summer?"

"Yes'm."

"May I see your pictures or are they private?"

Jess shoved his hair off his red forehead. "I'll show you 'um."

She smiled her beautiful even-toothed smile and shook her shining black hair back off her shoulders. "Great!" she said. "See you."

He nodded and smiled back. Even his toes had felt warm and tingly.

Now as he sat on the rug in the teachers' room the same warm feeling swept through him at the sound of her voice. Even her ordinary speaking voice bubbled up from inside her, rich and melodic.

Miss Edmunds fiddled a minute with her guitar, talking as she tightened the strings to the jingling of her bracelets and the thrumming of chords. She was in her jeans as usual and sat there cross-legged in front of them as though that was the way teachers always did. She asked a few of the kids how they were and how their summer had been. They kind of mumbled back. She didn't speak directly to Jess, but she gave him a look with those blue eyes of hers that made him zing like one of the strings she was strumming.

She took note of Leslie and asked for an introduction, which one of the girls prissily gave. Then she smiled at Leslie, and Leslie smiled back—the first time Jess could remember seeing Leslie smile since she won the race on Tuesday. "What do you like to sing, Leslie?"

"Oh, anything."

Miss Edmunds picked a few odd chords and then began to sing, more quietly than usual for that particular song:

> *"I see a land bright and clear*
> *And the time's coming near*
> *When we'll live in this land*
> *You and me, hand in hand . . ."*

People began to join in, quietly at first to match her mood, but as the song built up at the end, their voices did as well, so that by the time they got to the final "Free to be you and me," the whole school could hear them. Caught in the pure delight of it, Jess turned and his eyes met Leslie's. He smiled at her. What the heck? There wasn't any reason he couldn't. What was he scared of anyhow? Lord. Sometimes he acted like the original yellow-bellied sapsucker. He nodded and smiled again. She smiled back. He felt there in the teachers' room that it was the beginning of a new season in his life, and he chose deliberately to make it so.

He did not have to make any announcement to Leslie that he had changed his mind about her. She already knew it. She plunked herself down beside him on the bus and squeezed over closer to him to make room for May Belle on the same seat. She talked about Arlington, about the huge suburban school she used to go to with its gorgeous music room but not a single teacher in it as beautiful or as nice as Miss Edmunds.

"You had a gym?"

"Yeah. I think all the schools did. Or most of them anyway." She sighed. "I really miss it. I'm pretty good at gymnastics."

"I guess you hate it here."

"Yeah."

She was quiet for a moment, thinking, Jess decided, about

her former school, which he saw as bright and new with a gleaming gymnasium larger than the one at the consolidated high school.

"I guess you had a lot of friends there, too."

"Yeah."

"Why'd you come here?"

"My parents are reassessing their value structure."

"Huh?"

"They decided they were too hooked on money and success, so they bought that old farm and they're going to farm it and think about what's important."

Jess was staring at her with his mouth open. He knew it, and he couldn't help himself. It was the most ridiculous thing he had ever heard.

"But you're the one that's gotta pay."

"Yeah."

"Why don't they think about you?"

"We talked it over," she explained patiently. "I wanted to come, too." She looked past him out the window. "You never know ahead of time what something's really going to be like."

The bus had stopped. Leslie took May Belle's hand and led her off. Jess followed, still trying to figure out why two grown people and a smart girl like Leslie wanted to leave a comfortable life in the suburbs for a place like this.

They watched the bus roar off.

"You can't make a go of a farm nowadays, you know," he said finally. "My dad has to go to Washington to work, or we wouldn't have enough money . . ."

"Money is not the problem."

"Sure it's the problem."

"I mean," she said stiffly, "not for us."

It took him a minute to catch on. He did not know people

for whom money was not the problem. "Oh." He tried to remember not to talk about money with her after that.

But Leslie had other problems at Lark Creek that caused more of a rumpus than lack of money. There was the matter of television.

It started with Mrs. Myers reading out loud a composition that Leslie had written about her hobby. Everyone had had to write a paper about his or her favorite hobby. Jess had written about football, which he really hated, but he had enough brains to know that if he said drawing, everyone would laugh at him. Most of the boys swore that watching the Washington Redskins on TV was their favorite hobby. The girls were divided: those who didn't care much about what Mrs. Myers thought chose watching game shows on TV, and those like Wanda Kay Moore who were still aiming for A's chose reading Good Books. But Mrs. Myers didn't read anyone's paper out loud except Leslie's.

"I want to read this composition aloud. For two reasons. One, it is *beautifully* written. And two, it tells about an unusual hobby—for a girl." Mrs. Myers beamed her first-day smile at Leslie. Leslie stared at her desk. Being Mrs. Myers' pet was pure poison at Lark Creek. " 'Scuba Diving' by Leslie Burke."

Mrs. Myers' sharp voice cut Leslie's sentences into funny little phrases, but even so, the power of Leslie's words drew Jess with her under the dark water. Suddenly he could hardly breathe. Suppose you went under and your mask filled all up with water and you couldn't get to the top in time? He was choking and sweating. He tried to push down his panic. This was Leslie Burke's favorite hobby. Nobody would make up scuba diving to be their favorite hobby if it wasn't so. That meant Leslie did it a lot. That she wasn't scared of going deep,

deep down in a world of no air and little light. Lord, he was such a coward. How could he be all in a tremble just listening to Mrs. Myers read about it? He was worse a baby than Joyce Ann. His dad expected him to be a man. And here he was letting some girl who wasn't even ten yet scare the liver out of him by just telling what it was like to sight-see under water. Dumb, dumb, dumb.

"I am sure," Mrs. Myers was saying, "that all of you were as impressed as I was with Leslie's exciting essay."

Impressed. Lord. He'd nearly drowned.

In the classroom there was a shuffling of feet and papers. "Now I want to give you a homework assignment"—muffled groans—"that I'm sure you'll enjoy."—mumblings of unbelief—"Tonight on Channel 7 at 8 P.M. there is going to be a special about a famous underwater explorer—Jacques Cousteau. I want everyone to watch. Then write one page telling what you learned."

"A whole page?"

"Yes."

"Does spelling count?"

"Doesn't spelling always count, Gary?"

"Both sides of the paper?"

"One side will be enough, Wanda Kay. But I will give extra credit to those who do extra work."

Wanda Kay smiled primly. You could already see ten pages taking shape in her pointy head.

"Mrs. Myers."

"Yes, Leslie." Lord, Mrs. Myers was liable to crack her face if she kept up smiling like that.

"What if you can't watch the program?"

"You inform your parents that it is a homework assignment. I am sure they will not object."

"What if"—Leslie's voice faltered; then she shook her head

and cleared her throat so the words came out stronger—"what if you don't have a television set?"

Lord, Leslie. Don't say that. You can always watch on mine. But it was too late to save her. The hissing sounds of disbelief were already building into a rumbling of contempt.

Mrs. Myers blinked her eyes. "Well. Well." She blinked some more. You could tell she was trying to figure out how to save Leslie, too. "Well. In that case one could write a one-page composition on something else. Couldn't one, Leslie?" She tried to smile across the classroom upheaval to Leslie, but it was no use. "Class! Class! *Class!*" Her Leslie smile shifted suddenly and ominously into a scowl that silenced the storm.

She handed out dittoed sheets of arithmetic problems. Jess stole a look at Leslie. Her face, bent low over the math sheet, was red and fierce.

At recess time when he was playing King of the Mountain, he could see that Leslie was surrounded by a group of girls led by Wanda Kay. He couldn't hear what they were saying, but he could tell by the proud way Leslie was throwing her head back that the others were making fun of her. Greg Williams grabbed him then, and while they wrestled, Leslie disappeared. It was none of his business, really, but he threw Greg down the hill as hard as he could and yelled to no one in particular, "Gotta go."

He stationed himself across from the girls' room. Leslie came out in a few minutes. He could tell she had been crying.

"Hey, Leslie," he called softly.

"Go away!" She turned abruptly and headed the other way in a fast walk. With an eye on the office door, he ran after her. Nobody was supposed to be in the halls during recess. "Leslie. Whatsa matter?"

"You know perfectly well what's the matter, Jess Aarons."

"Yeah." He rubbed his hair. "If you'd justa kept your mouth shut. You can always watch at my . . ."

But she had wheeled around again, and was zooming down the hall. Before he could finish the sentence and catch up with her, she was swinging the door to the girls' room right at his nose. Jess slunk out of the building. He couldn't risk Mr. Turner catching him hanging around the girls' room as though he was some kind of pervert or something.

After school Leslie got on the bus before he did and went straight to the corner of the long back seat—right to the seventh graders' seat. He jerked his head at her to warn her to come farther up front, but she wouldn't even look at him. He could see the seventh graders headed for the bus—the huge bossy bosomy girls and the mean, skinny, narrow-eyed boys. They'd kill her for sitting in their territory. He jumped up and ran to the back and grabbed Leslie by the arm. "You gotta come up to your regular seat, Leslie."

Even as he spoke, he could feel the bigger kids pushing up behind him down the narrow aisle. Indeed, Janice Avery, who among all the seventh graders was the one person who devoted her entire life to scaring the wits out of anyone smaller than she, was right behind him. "Move, kid," she said.

He planted his body as firmly as he could, although his heart was knocking at his Adam's apple. "C'mon, Leslie," he said, and then he made himself turn and give Janice Avery one of those look-overs from frizz blond hair, past too tight blouse and broad-beamed jeans, to gigantic sneakers. When he finished, he swallowed, stared straight up into her scowling face, and said, almost steadily, "Don't look like there'll be room across the back here for you *and* Janice Avery."

Somebody hooted. "Weight Watchers is waiting for you, Janice!"

Janice's eyes were hate-mad, but she moved aside for Jess and Leslie to make their way past her to their regular seat.

Leslie glanced back as they sat down, and then leaned over. "She's going to get you for that, Jess. Boy, she is mad."

Jess warmed to the tone of respect in Leslie's voice, but he didn't dare look back. "Heck," he said. "You think I'm going to let some dumb cow like that scare me?"

By the time they got off the bus, he could finally send a swallow past his Adam's apple without choking. He even gave a little wave at the back seat as the bus pulled off.

Leslie was grinning at him over May Belle's head.

"Well," he said happily. "See you."

"Hey, do you think we could do something this afternoon?"

"Me, too! I wanna do something, too," May Belle shrilled.

Jess looked at Leslie. No was in her eyes. "Not this time, May Belle. Leslie and I got something we gotta do just by ourselves today. You can carry my books home and tell Momma I'm over at Burkes'. OK?"

"You ain't got nothing to do. You ain't even planned nothing."

Leslie came and leaned over May Belle, putting her hand on the little girl's thin shoulder. "May Belle, would you like some new paper dolls?"

May Belle slid her eyes around suspiciously. "What kind?"

"Life in Colonial America."

May Belle shook her head. "I want Bride or Miss America."

"You can pretend these are bride paper dolls. They have lots of beautiful long dresses."

"Whatsa matter with 'um?"

"Nothing. They're brand-new."

"How come you don't want 'um if they're so great?"

"When you're my age"—Leslie gave a little sigh—"you just

don't play with paper dolls anymore. My grandmother sent me these. You know how it is, grandmothers just forget you're growing up."

May Belle's one living grandmother was in Georgia and never sent her anything. "You already punched 'um out?"

"No, honestly. And all the clothes punch out, too. You don't have to use scissors."

They could see she was weakening. "How about," Jess began, "you coming down and taking a look at 'um, and if they suit you, you could take 'um along home when you go tell Momma where I am?"

After they had watched May Belle tearing up the hill, clutching her new treasure, Jess and Leslie turned and ran up over the empty field behind the old Perkins place and down to the dry creek bed that separated farmland from the woods. There was an old crab apple tree there, just at the bank of the creek bed, from which someone long forgotten had hung a rope.

They took turns swinging across the gully on the rope. It was a glorious autumn day, and if you looked up as you swung, it gave you the feeling of floating. Jess leaned back and drank in the rich, clear color of the sky. He was drifting, drifting like a fat white lazy cloud back and forth across the blue.

"Do you know what we need?" Leslie called to him. Intoxicated as he was with the heavens, he couldn't imagine needing anything on earth.

"We need a place," she said, "just for us. It would be so secret that we would never tell anyone in the whole world about it." Jess came swinging back and dragged his feet to stop. She lowered her voice almost to a whisper. "It might be a whole secret country," she continued, "and you and I would be the rulers of it."

Her words stirred inside of him. He'd like to be a ruler of something. Even something that wasn't real. "OK," he said. "Where could we have it?"

"Over there in the woods where nobody would come and mess it up."

There were parts of the woods that Jess did not like. Dark places where it was almost like being under water, but he didn't say so.

"I know"—she was getting excited—"it could be a magic country like Narnia, and the only way you can get in is by swinging across on this enchanted rope." Her eyes were bright. She grabbed the rope. "Come on," she said. "Let's find a place to build our castle stronghold."

They had gone only a few yards into the woods beyond the creek bed when Leslie stopped.

"How about right here?" she asked.

"Sure," Jess agreed quickly, relieved that there was no need to plunge deeper into the woods. He would take her there, of course, for he wasn't such a coward that he would mind a little exploring now and then farther in amongst the ever-darkening columns of the tall pines. But as a regular thing, as a permanent place, this was where he would choose to be—here where the dogwood and redbud played hide and seek between the oaks and evergreens, and the sun flung itself in golden streams through the trees to splash warmly at their feet.

"Sure," he repeated himself, nodding vigorously. The underbrush was dry and would be easy to clear away. The ground was almost level. "This'll be a good place to build."

Leslie named their secret land "Terabithia," and she loaned

Jess all of her books about Narnia, so he would know how things went in a magic kingdom—how the animals and the trees must be protected and how a ruler must behave. That was the hard part. When Leslie spoke, the words rolling out so regally, you knew she was a proper queen. He could hardly manage English, much less the poetic language of a king.

But he could make stuff. They dragged boards and other materials down from the scrap heap by Miss Bessie's pasture and built their castle stronghold in the place they had found in the woods. Leslie filled a three-pound coffee can with crackers and dried fruit and a one-pound can with strings and nails. They found five old Pepsi bottles which they washed and filled with water, in case, as Leslie said, "of siege."

Like God in the Bible, they looked at what they had made and found it very good.

"You should draw a picture of Terabithia for us to hang in the castle," Leslie said.

"I can't." How could he explain it in a way Leslie would understand, how he yearned to reach out and capture the quivering life about him and how when he tried, it slipped past his fingertips, leaving a dry fossil upon the page? "I just can't get the poetry of the trees," he said.

She nodded. "Don't worry," she said. "You will someday."

He believed her because there in the shadowy light of the stronghold everything seemed possible. Between the two of them they owned the world and no enemy, Gary Fulcher, Wanda Kay Moore, Janice Avery, Jess's own fears and insufficiencies, nor any of the foes whom Leslie imagined attacking Terabithia, could ever really defeat them.

A few days after they finished the castle, Janice Avery fell down in the school bus and yelled that Jess had tripped her as she went past. She made such a fuss that Mrs. Prentice, the driver, ordered Jess off the bus, and he had to walk the three miles home.

When Jess finally got to Terabithia, Leslie was huddled next to one of the cracks below the roof trying to get enough light to read. There was a picture on the cover which showed a killer whale attacking a dolphin.

"Whatcha doing?" He came in and sat beside her on the ground.

"Reading. I had to do something. That girl!" Her anger came rocketing to the surface.

"It don't matter. I don't mind walking all that much." What was a little hike compared to what Janice Avery might have chosen to do?

"It's the *principle* of the thing, Jess. That's what you've got to understand. You have to stop people like that. Otherwise they turn into tyrants and dictators."

He reached over and took the whale book from her hands, pretending to study the bloody picture on the jacket. "Getting any good ideas?"

"What?"

"I thought you was getting some ideas on how to stop Janice Avery."

"No, stupid. We're trying to *save* the whales. They might become extinct."

He gave her back the book. "You save the whales and shoot the people, huh?"

She grinned finally. "Something like that, I guess. Say, did you ever hear the story about Moby Dick?"

"Who's that?"

"Well, there was once this huge white whale named Moby Dick. . . ." And Leslie began to spin out a wonderful story about a whale and a crazy sea captain who was bent on killing it. His fingers itched to try to draw it on paper. Maybe if he had some proper paints, he could do it. There ought to be a way of making the whale shimmering white against the dark water.

At first they avoided each other during school hours, but by October they grew careless about their friendship. Gary Fulcher, like Brenda, took great pleasure in teasing Jess about his "*girl* friend." It hardly bothered Jess. He knew that a *girl* friend was somebody who chased you on the playground and tried to grab you and kiss you. He could no more imagine Leslie chasing a boy than he could imagine Mrs. Double-Chinned Myers shinnying up the flagpole. Gary Fulcher could go to you-know-where and warm his toes.

There was really no free time at school except recess, and now that there were no races, Jess and Leslie usually looked for a quiet place on the field, and sat and talked. Except for the magic half hour on Fridays, recess was all that Jess looked forward to at school. Leslie could always come up with something funny that made the long days bearable. Often the joke was on Mrs. Myers. Leslie was one of those people who sat quietly at her desk, never whispering or day-dreaming or chewing gum, doing beautiful schoolwork, and yet her brain was so full of mischief that if the teacher could have once seen through that mask of perfection, she would have thrown her out in horror.

Jess could hardly keep a straight face in class just trying to imagine what might be going on behind that angelic look of

Leslie's. One whole morning, as Leslie had related it at recess, she had spent imagining Mrs. Myers on one of those fat farms down in Arizona. In her fantasy, Mrs. Myers was one of the foodaholics who would hide bits of candy bars in odd places —up the hot water faucet!—only to be found out and publicly humiliated before all the other fat ladies. That afternoon Jess kept having visions of Mrs. Myers dressed only in a pink corset being weighed in. "You've been cheating again, Gussie!" the tall skinny directoress was saying. Mrs. Myers was on the verge of tears.

"Jesse Aarons!" The teacher's sharp voice punctured his daydream. He couldn't look Mrs. Myers straight in her pudgy face. He'd crack up. He set his sight on her uneven hemline.

"Yes'm." He was going to have to get coaching from Leslie. Mrs. Myers always caught him when his mind was on vacation, but she never seemed to suspect Leslie of not paying attention. He sneaked a glance up that way. Leslie was totally absorbed in her geography book, or so it would appear to anyone who didn't know.

Terabithia was cold in November. They didn't dare build a fire in the castle, though sometimes they would build one outside and huddle around it. For a while Leslie had been able to keep two sleeping bags in the stronghold, but around the first of December her father noticed their absence, and she had to take them back. Actually, Jess made her take them back. It was not that he was afraid of the Burkes exactly. Leslie's parents were young, with straight white teeth and lots of hair—both of them. Leslie called them Judy and Bill, which bothered Jess more than he wanted it to. It was none of his business what Leslie called her parents. But he just couldn't get used to it.

Both of the Burkes were writers. Mrs. Burke wrote novels and, according to Leslie, was more famous than Mr. Burke, who wrote about politics. It was really something to see the shelf that had their books on it. Mrs. Burke was "Judith Hancock" on the cover, which threw you at first, but then if you looked on the back, there was her picture looking very young and serious. Mr. Burke was going back and forth to Washington to finish a book he was working on with someone else, but he had promised Leslie that after Christmas he would stay home and fix up the house and plant his garden and listen to music and read books out loud and write only in his spare time.

They didn't look like Jess's idea of rich, but even he could tell that the jeans they wore had not come off the counter at Newberry's. There was no TV at the Burkes', but there were mountains of records and a stereo set that looked like something off *Star Trek*. And although their car was small and dusty, it was Italian and looked expensive, too.

They were always nice to Jess when he went over, but then they would suddenly begin talking about French politics or string quartets (which he at first thought was a square box made out of string), or how to save the timber wolves or redwoods or singing whales, and he was scared to open his mouth and show once and for all how dumb he was.

He wasn't comfortable having Leslie at his house either. Joyce Ann would stare, her index finger pulling down her mouth and making her drool. Brenda and Ellie always managed some remark about "*girl* friend." His mother acted stiff and funny just the way she did when she had to go up to school about something. Later she would refer to Leslie's "tacky" clothes. Leslie always wore pants, even to school. Her hair was "shorter than a boy's." Her parents were "hardly more than hippies." May Belle either tried to push in with him and Leslie or sulked at being left out. His father had seen Leslie only a few times and had nodded to show that he had noticed her, but his mother said that she was sure he was fretting that his only son did nothing but play with girls, and they both were worried about what would become of it.

Jess didn't concern himself with what would "become of it." For the first time in his life he got up every morning with something to look forward to. Leslie was more than his friend. She was his other, more exciting self—his way to Terabithia and all the worlds beyond.

Terabithia was their secret, which was a good thing, for how could Jess have ever explained it to an outsider? Just walking down the hill toward the woods made something warm and liquid steal through his body. The closer he came to the dry creek bed and the crab apple tree rope the more he could feel the beating of his heart. He grabbed the end of the rope and swung out toward the other bank with a kind of wild exhilaration and landed gently on his feet, taller and stronger and wiser in that mysterious land.

Leslie's favorite place besides the castle stronghold was the pine forest. There the trees grew so thick at the top that the sunshine was veiled. No low bush or grass could grow in that dim light, so the ground was carpeted with golden needles.

"I used to think this place was haunted," Jess had confessed to Leslie the first afternoon he had revved up his courage to bring her there.

"Oh, but it is," she said. "But you don't have to be scared. It's not haunted with evil things."

"How do you know?"

"You can just feel it. Listen."

At first he heard only the stillness. It was the stillness that had always frightened him before, but this time it was like the moment after Miss Edmunds finished a song, just after the chords hummed down to silence. Leslie was right. They stood there, not moving, not wanting the swish of dry needles beneath their feet to break the spell. Far away from their former world came the cry of geese heading southward.

Leslie took a deep breath. "This is not an ordinary place," she whispered. "Even the rulers of Terabithia come into it only at times of greatest sorrow or of greatest joy. We must strive to keep it sacred. It would not do to disturb the Spirits."

He nodded, and without speaking, they went back to the creek bank where they shared together a solemn meal of crackers and dried fruit.

The Giant Killers

Leslie liked to make up stories about the giants that threatened the peace of Terabithia, but they both knew that the real giant in their lives was Janice Avery. Of course, it wasn't only Jess and Leslie that she was after. She had two friends, Wilma Dean and Bobby Sue Henshaw, who were almost as big as she was, and the three of them would roam the playground, grabbing up hopscotch rocks, running through jump ropes, and laughing while second graders screamed. They would even stand outside the girls' room first thing every morning and make the little girls give them their milk money before they'd let them go to the bathroom.

May Belle, unfortunately, was a slow learner. Her daddy had brought her a package of Twinkies, and she was so proud that as soon as she got on the bus she forgot everything she knew and yelled to another first grader, "Guess what I got in my lunch today, Billy Jean?"

"What?"

"Twinkies!" she shouted so loud you could have heard her in the back seat even if you were deaf in both ears. Out of the corner of his eye, Jess thought he saw Janice Avery perk up.

When they sat down, May Belle was still screeching about her dadgum Twinkies over the roar of the motor. "My daddy brung 'um to me from Washington!"

Jess threw another look at the back seat. "You better shut up about those dang Twinkies," he said in her ear.

"You just jealous 'cause Daddy didn't bring you none."

"OK." He shrugged across her head at Leslie to say *I warned her, didn't I*? and Leslie nodded back.

Neither of them was too surprised to see May Belle come screaming toward them at recess time.

"She stole my Twinkies!"

Jess sighed. "May Belle, didn't I tell you?"

"You gotta kill Janice Avery. Kill her! Kill her! Kill her!"

"*Shhh,*" Leslie said, stroking May Belle's head, but May Belle didn't want comfort, she wanted revenge.

"You gotta beat her up into a million pieces!"

He'd sooner tangle with Mrs. Godzilla herself. "Fighting ain't gonna get back nothing, May Belle. Them Twinkies is well on the way to padding Janice Avery's bottom by now."

Leslie snickered, but May Belle was not to be distracted. "You're just yeller, Jesse Aarons. If you wasn't yeller, you'd beat somebody up if they took your little sister's Twinkies." She broke into a fresh round of sobbing.

Jess stiffened. He avoided Leslie's eyes. Lord, there was no escape. He'd have to fight the female gorilla now.

"Look, May Belle," Leslie was saying. "If Jess picks a fight with Janice Avery, you know perfectly well what will happen."

May Belle wiped her nose on the back of her hand. "She'll beat him up."

"Noooo. *He'll* get kicked out of school for fighting a girl. You know how Mr. Turner is about boys who pick on girls."

"She stole my Twinkies."

"I know she did, May Belle. And Jess and I are going to figure out a way to pay her back for it. Aren't we Jess?"

He nodded vigorously. Anything was better than promising to fight Janice Avery.

"Whatcha gonna do?"

"I don't know yet. We'll have to plan it out very carefully, but I promise you, May Belle, we'll get her."

"Cross-your-heart-and-hope-to-die?"

Leslie solemnly crossed her heart. May Belle turned expectantly to Jess, so he crossed his, too, trying hard not to feel like a fool, crossing his heart to a first grader in the middle of the playground.

May Belle snuffled loudly. "It ain't as good as seeing her beat to a million pieces."

"No," said Leslie, "I'm sure it isn't, but with Mr. Turner running this school, it's the best we can do, right, Jess?"

"Right."

That afternoon, crouched in the stronghold of Terabithia, they held a council of war. How to get Janice Avery without ending up squashed or suspended—that was their problem.

"Maybe we could get her caught doing something." Leslie was trying out another idea after they had both rejected putting honey on her bus seat and glue in her hand lotion. "You know she smokes in the girls' room. If we could just get Mr. Turner to walk past while the smoke is pouring out—"

Jess shook his head hopelessly. "It wouldn't take her five minutes to find out who squawked." There was a moment of silence while they both considered what Janice Avery might do to anyone who reported her to the principal. "We gotta get her without her knowing who done it."

"Yeah." Leslie chewed away at a dried apricot. "You know what girls like Janice hate most?"

"What?"

"Being made a fool of."

Jess remembered how Janice had looked that day he'd made everyone laugh at her on the bus. Leslie was right. There was a crack in the old hippo hide. "Yeah." He nodded, beginning to smile. "Yeah. Do we get her about being fat?"

"How about," Leslie began slowly, "how about boys? Who's she stuck on?"

"Willard Hughes, I reckon. Every girl in the seventh grade slides to the ground when he walks by."

"Yeah." Leslie's eyes were shining. The plan came all in a rush. "We write her a note, you see, and pretend it's from Willard."

Jess was already getting a pencil from the can and yanking a piece of notebook paper out from under a rock. He handed them to Leslie.

"No, you write. My handwriting is too good for Willard Hughes."

He got set and waited.

"OK," she said. "Um. 'Dear Janice.' No. 'Dearest Janice.' "

Jess hesitated, doubtful.

"Believe me, Jess. She'll eat it up. OK. 'Dearest Janice.' Don't worry about punctuation or anything. We have to make it look as if Willard Hughes really wrote it. OK. 'Dearest Janice, Maybe you won't believe me, but I love you.' "

"You think she'll . . . ?" he asked as he wrote it down.

"I told you, she'll eat it up. Girls like Janice Avery believe just what they want to in this kind of situation. OK, now. 'If you say you do not love me, it will break my heart. So please don't. If you love me as much as I love you, my darling—' "

"Hold it. I can't write that fast."

Leslie waited, and when he looked up, she continued in a moony voice, " 'Meet me behind the school this afternoon after school. Do not worry about missing your bus. I want to walk home with you and talk about US'—put 'us' in capitals —'my darling. Love and kisses, Willard Hughes.' "

"Kisses?"

"Yeah, kisses. Put a little row of x's in there, too." She paused, looking over his shoulder while he finished. "Oh, yes. Put 'P.S.' "

He did.

"Um. 'Don't tell any—don't tell *no*body. Let our love be a secret for only us two right now.' "

"Why'cha put that in?"

"So she'll be sure to tell somebody, stupid." Leslie reread the note, nodding approval. "Good. You misspelled 'believe' and 'two.' " She studied it a minute longer. "Gee, I'm pretty good at this."

"Sure. You probably had some big secret love down in Arlington."

"Jess Aarons, I'm going to kill you."

"Hey, girl, you kill the king of Terabithia, and you're in trouble."

"Regicide," she said proudly.

"Regi-what?"

"Did I ever tell you the story of Hamlet?"

He rolled over on his back. "Not yet," he said happily. Lord, he loved Leslie's stories. Someday, when he was good enough, he would ask her to write them in a book and let him do all the pictures.

"Well," she began, "there was once a prince of Denmark, named Hamlet. . . ."

In his head he drew the shadowy castle with the tortured prince pacing the parapets. How could you make a ghost come out of the fog? Crayons wouldn't do, of course, but with paints you could put one thin color on top of another so that you would begin to see a pale figure moving from deep inside the paper. He began to shiver. He knew he could do it if Leslie would let him use her paints.

❦

The hardest part of the plan to get Janice Avery was to plant the note. They sneaked into the building the next morning before the first bell. Leslie went several yards ahead so that if they were caught, no one would think they were together. Mr. Turner was death on boys and girls he caught sneaking around the halls together. She got to the door of the seventh-grade classroom and peeked in. Then she signaled Jess to come ahead. The hairs prickled up his neck. Lord.

"How'll I find her desk?"

"I thought you knew where she sat."

He shook his head.

"I guess you'll have to look in every one until you find it. Hurry. I'll be lookout for you." She closed the door quietly and left him shuffling through each desk, trying to be careful not to make a mess, but his stupid hands were shaking so much he could hardly pull anything out to look for names.

Suddenly he heard Leslie's voice. "Oh, *Mrs. Pierce*, I've just been standing here *waiting* for you."

Lord. The seventh-grade teacher was right out there in the hall, heading for this room. He stood frozen. He couldn't hear what Mrs. Pierce was saying back to Leslie through the closed door.

"Yes, ma'am. There is a very interesting nest on the south end of the building, and since"—Leslie raised her voice even louder—"you know so much about science, I was hoping you could take a minute *to look at it with me* and tell me what built it."

There was the mumble of a reply.

"Oh, *thank you*, Mrs. Pierce"—Leslie was practically screaming—"It won't take but a *minute*, and it would mean so much to me!"

As soon as he heard their retreating footsteps, he flew around the remaining desks until, oh, joy, he found one with a composition book that had Janice Avery's name on it. He stuffed the note on top of everything else inside the desk and raced out of the room to the boys' room, where he hid in one of the stalls until the bell rang to go to homeroom.

At recess time Janice Avery was in a tight huddle with Wilma and Bobby Sue. Then, instead of teasing the little girls, the three of them wandered off arm in arm to watch the big boys' football. As the trio passed them, Jess could see Janice's face all pink and prideful. He rolled his eyes at Leslie, and she rolled hers back at him.

As the bus was about to pull out that afternoon, one of the seventh-grade boys, Billy Morris, yelled up to Mrs. Prentice that Janice Avery wasn't on the bus yet.

"It's OK, Miz Prentice," Wilma Dean called up. "She ain't riding this evening." Then in a loud whisper, "Reckon you all know that Janice has a heavy date with you know who."

"Who?" asked Billy.

"Willard Hughes. He's so crazy about her he can't hardly stand it. He's even walking her all the way home."

"Yeah? Well the 304 just pulled out with Willard Hughes on the back seat. If he's got a big date, he don't seem to know much about it."

"You lie, Billy Morris!"

Billy yelled a cuss word, and the entire back seat plunged into a heated discussion as to whether Janice Avery and Willard Hughes were or were not in love and were or were not seeing each other secretly.

As Billy got off the bus, he hollered to Wilma, "You just better tell Janice that Willard is gonna be mad when he hears what she's spreading all over the school!"

Wilma's face was crimson as she screamed out the window, "OK, you dummy! You talk to Willard. You'll see. Just ask him about that letter! You'll see!"

"Poor old Janice Avery," Jess said as they sat in the castle later.

"Poor old Janice? She deserves everything she gets and then some!"

"I reckon." He sighed. "But, still—"

Leslie looked stricken. "You're not sorry we did it, are you?"

"No. I reckon we had to do it, but still—"

"Still what?"

He grinned. "Maybe I got this thing for Janice like you got this thing for killer whales."

She punched him in the shoulder. "Let's go out and find some giants or walking dead to fight. I'm sick of Janice Avery."

The next day Janice Avery stomped onto the bus, her eyes daring everyone in sight to say a word. Leslie nudged May Belle.

May Belle's eyes went wide. "Did 'cha—?"

"*Shhh.* Yes."

May Belle turned completely around and stared at the back seat; then she turned back and poked Jess. "You made her *that* mad?"

Jess nodded, trying to move his head as little as possible as he did so.

"We wrote that letter," Leslie whispered. "But you mustn't tell anyone, or she'll kill us."

"I know," said May Belle, her eyes shining. "I know."

The Coming of Prince Terrien

Christmas was almost a month away, but at Jess's house the girls were already obsessed with it. This year Ellie and Brenda both had boyfriends at the consolidated high school and the problem of what to give them and what to expect from them was cause of endless speculation and fights. Fights, because as usual, their mother was complaining that there was hardly enough money to give the little girls something from Santa Claus, let alone a surplus to buy record albums or shirts for a pair of boys she'd never set eyes on.

"What are you giving your girl friend, Jess?" Brenda screwed her face up in that ugly way she had. He tried to ignore her. He was reading one of Leslie's books, and the adventures of an assistant pig keeper were far more important to him than Brenda's sauce.

"Don't you know, Brenda?" Ellie joined in. "Jess ain't got no *girl* friend."

"Well, you're right for once. Nobody with any sense would call that stick a *girl*." Brenda pushed her face right into his and grinned the word "girl" through her big painted lips. Something huge and hot swelled right up inside of him, and if he hadn't jumped out of the chair and walked away, he would have smacked her.

He tried to figure out later what had made him so angry. Partly, of course, it made him furious that anyone as dumb as Brenda would think she could make fun of Leslie. Lord, it hurt his guts to realize that it was Brenda who was his blood sister, and that really, from anyone else's point of view, he and Leslie were not related at all. Maybe, he thought, I was a foundling, like in the stories. Way back when the creek had water in it, I came floating down it in a wicker basket waterproofed with pitch. My dad found me and brought me here because he'd always wanted a son and just had stupid daughters. My real parents and brothers and sisters live far away— farther away than West Virginia or even Ohio. Somewhere I have a family who have rooms filled with nothing but books and who still grieve for their baby who was stolen.

He shook himself back to the source of his anger. He was angry, too, because it would soon be Christmas and he had nothing to give Leslie. It was not that she would expect something expensive; it was that he needed to give her something as much as he needed to eat when he was hungry.

He thought about making her a book of his drawings. He even stole paper and crayons from school to do it with. But nothing he drew seemed good enough, and he would end up scrawling across the half-finished page and poking it into the stove to burn up.

By the last week of school before the holiday, he was growing desperate. There was no one he could ask for help or advice. His dad had told him he would give him a dollar for each member of the family, but even if he cheated on the family presents, there was no way he could get from that enough to buy Leslie anything worth giving her. Besides, May Belle had her heart set on a Barbie doll, and he had already promised to pool his money with Ellie and Brenda for that. Then the price had gone up, and he found he would have to go over into every one else's dollar to make up the full amount for May Belle. Somehow this year May Belle needed something special. She was always moping around. He and Leslie couldn't include her in their activities, but that was hard to explain to someone like May Belle. Why didn't she play with Joyce Ann? He couldn't be expected to entertain her all the time. Still— still, she ought to have the Barbie.

So there was no money, and he seemed paralyzed in his efforts to make anything for Leslie. She wouldn't be like Brenda or Ellie. She wouldn't laugh at him no matter what he gave her. But for his own sake he had to give her something that he could be proud of.

If he had the money, he'd buy her a TV. One of those tiny Japanese ones that she could keep in her own room without bothering Judy and Bill. It didn't seem fair with all their money that they'd gotten rid of the TV. It wasn't as if Leslie would watch the way Brenda did—with her mouth open and her eyes bulging like a goldfish, hour after hour. But every once in a while, a person liked to watch. At least if she had one, it would be one less thing for the kids at school to sneer about. But, of course, there was no way that he could buy her a TV. It was pretty stupid of him even to think about it.

Lord, he was stupid. He gazed miserably out the window of the school bus. It was a wonder someone like Leslie would even give him the time of day. It was because there was no

one else. If she had found anyone else at that dumb school—
he was so stupid he had almost gone straight past the sign
without catching on. But something in a corner of his head
clicked, and he jumped up, pushing past Leslie and May Belle.

"See you later," he mumbled, and shoved his way up the
aisle through pair after pair of sprawling legs.

"Lemme off here, Miz Prentice, will you?"

"This ain't your stop."

"Gotta do an errand for my mother," he lied.

" 'Long as you don't get me into trouble." She eased the
brakes.

"No'm. Thanks."

He swung off the bus before it had really stopped and ran
back toward the sign.

"Puppies," it said. "Free."

❧

Jess told Leslie to meet him at the castle stronghold on
Christmas Eve afternoon. The rest of his family had gone to
the Millsburg Plaza for last-minute shopping, but he stayed
behind. The dog was a little brown-and-black thing with great
brown eyes. Jess stole a ribbon from Brenda's drawer, and
hurried across the field and down the hill with the puppy
squirming in his arms. Before he got to the creek bed, it had
licked his face raw and sent a stream down his jacket front,
but he couldn't be mad. He tucked it tightly under his arm and
swung across the creek as gently as he could. He could have
walked through the gully. It would have been easier, but he
couldn't escape the feeling that one must enter Terabithia only
by the prescribed entrance. He couldn't let the puppy break
the rules. It might mean bad luck for both of them.

At the stronghold he tied the ribbon around the puppy's

neck, laughing as it backed out of the loop and chewed at the ends of the ribbon. It was a clever, lively little thing—a present Jess could be proud of.

There was no mistaking the delight in Leslie's eyes. She dropped to her knees on the cold ground, picked the puppy up, and held it close to her face.

"Watch it," Jess cautioned. "It sprays worse'n a water pistol."

Leslie moved it out a little way. "Is it male or female?"

Once in a rare while there was something he could teach Leslie. "Boy," he said happily.

"Then we'll name him Prince Terrien and make him the guardian of Terabithia."

She put the puppy down and got to her feet.

"Where you going?"

"To the grove of the pines," she answered. "This is a time of greatest joy."

Later that afternoon Leslie gave Jess his present. It was a

box of watercolors with twenty-four tubes of color and three brushes and a pad of heavy art paper.

"Lord," he said. "Thank you." He tried to think of a better way to say it, but he couldn't. "Thank you," he repeated.

"It's not a great present like yours," she said humbly, "but I hope you'll like it."

He wanted to tell her how proud and good she made him feel, that the rest of Christmas didn't matter because today had been so good, but the words he needed weren't there. "Oh, yeah, yeah," he said, and then got up on his knees and began to bark at Prince Terrien. The puppy raced around him in circles, yelping with delight.

Leslie began to laugh. It egged Jess on. Everything the dog did, he imitated, flopping down at last with his tongue lolling out. Leslie was laughing so hard she had trouble getting the words out. "You—you're crazy. How will we teach him to be a noble guardian? You're turning him into a clown."

"*R-r-r-oof,*" wailed Prince Terrien, rolling his eyes skyward. Jess and Leslie both collapsed. They were in pain from the laughter.

"Maybe," said Leslie at last. "We'd better make him court jester."

"What about his name?"

"Oh, we'll let him keep his name. Even a prince"—this in her most Terabithian voice—"even a prince may be a fool."

That night the glow of the afternoon stayed with him. Even his sisters' squabbling about when presents were to be opened did not touch him. He helped May Belle wrap her wretched little gifts and even sang "Santa Claus Is Coming to Town" with her and Joyce Ann. Then Joyce Ann cried because they had no fireplace and Santa wouldn't be able to find the way, and suddenly he felt sorry for her going to Millsburg Plaza and seeing all those things and hoping that some guy in a red suit would give her all her dreams. May Belle at six was already too wise. She was just hoping for that stupid Barbie. He was glad he'd splurged on it. Joyce Ann wouldn't care that he only had a hair clip for her. She would blame Santa, not him, for being cheap.

He put his arm awkwardly around Joyce Ann. "C'mon Joyce Ann. Don't cry. Old Santa knows the way. He don't need a chimney, does he, May Belle?" May Belle was watching him with her big, solemn eyes. Jess gave her a knowing wink over Joyce Ann's head. It melted her.

"Naw, Joyce Ann. He knows the way. He knows everything." She squenched up her right cheek in a vain effort to return his wink. She was a good kid. He really liked old May Belle.

The next morning he helped her dress and undress her Barbie at least thirty times. Slithering the skinny dress over the doll's head and arms and snapping the tiny fasteners was more than her chubby six-year-old fingers could manage.

He had received a racing car set, which he tried to run to please his father. It wasn't one of those big sets that they advertised on TV, but it was electric, and he knew his dad had put more money into it than he should have. But the silly cars kept falling off at the curves until his father was cursing at them with impatience. Jess wanted it to be OK. He wanted so much for his dad to be proud of his present, the way he, Jess, had been proud of the puppy.

"It's really great. Really. I just ain't got the hang of it yet." His face was red, and he kept shoving his hair back out of his eyes as he leaned over the plastic figure-eight track.

"Cheap junk." His father kicked at the floor dangerously near the track. "Don't get nothing for your money these days."

Joyce Ann was lying on her bed screaming because she had yanked the string out of her talking doll and it was no longer talking. Brenda had her lip stuck out because Ellie had gotten a pair of panty hose in her Christmas stocking and she had only bobby socks. Ellie wasn't helping matters, prancing around in her new hose, making a big show of helping Momma with the ham and sweet potatoes for dinner. Lord, sometimes Ellie was as snotty as Wanda Kay Moore.

"Jesse Oliver Aarons, Jr., if you can stop playing with those fool cars long enough to milk the cow, I'd be most appreciative. Miss Bessie don't take no holiday, even if you do."

Jess jumped up, pleased for an excuse to leave the track which he couldn't make work to his dad's satisfaction. His mother seemed not to notice the promptness of his response but went on in a complaining voice, "I don't know what I'd do without Ellie. She's the only one of you kids ever cares whether I live or die." Ellie smiled like a plastic angel first at Jess and then at Brenda, who glared back.

Leslie must have been watching for him because as soon as he started across the yard he could see her running out of the old Perkins place, the puppy half tripping her as it chased circles around her.

They met at Miss Bessie's shed. "I thought you'd never come out this morning."

"Yeah, well, Christmas, you know."

Prince Terrien began to snap at Miss Bessie's hooves. She stamped in annoyance. Leslie picked him up, so Jess could milk. The puppy squirmed and licked, making it almost impossible for her to talk. She giggled happily. "Dumb dog," she said proudly.

"Yeah." It felt like Christmas again.

SEVEN

The Golden Room

Mr. Burke had begun to repair the old Perkins place. After Christmas, Mrs. Burke was right in the middle of writing a book, so she wasn't available to help, which left Leslie the jobs of hunting and fetching. For all his smartness with politics and music, Mr. Burke was inclined to be absent-minded. He would put down the hammer to pick up the "How to" book and then lose the hammer between there and the project he was working on. Leslie was good at finding things for him, and he liked her company as well. When she came home from school and on the weekends, he wanted her around. Leslie explained all this to Jess.

Jess tried going to Terabithia alone, but it was no good. It needed Leslie to make the magic. He was afraid he would destroy everything by trying to force the magic on his own, when it was plain that the magic was reluctant to come for him.

If he went home, either his mother was after him to do

some chore or May Belle wanted him to play Barbie. Lord, he wished a million times he'd never helped buy that stupid doll. He'd no more than lie down on the floor to paint than May Belle would be after him to put an arm back on or snap up a dress. Joyce Ann was worse. She got a devilish delight out of sitting smack down on his rump when he was stretched out working. If he yelled at her to get the heck off him, she'd stick her index finger in the corner of her mouth and holler. Which would, of course, crank up his mother.

"Jesse Oliver! You leave that baby alone. Whatcha mean lying there in the middle of the floor doing nothing anyway? Didn't I tell you I couldn't cook supper before you chopped wood for the stove?"

Sometimes he would sneak down to the old Perkins place and find Prince Terrien crying on the porch, where Mr. Burke had exiled him. You couldn't blame the man. No one could get anything done with that animal grabbing his hand or jumping up to lick his face. He'd take P. T. for a romp in the Burkes' upper field. If it was a mild day, Miss Bessie would be mooing nervously from across the fence. She couldn't seem to get used to the yipping and snapping. Or maybe it was the time of year—the last dregs of winter spoiling the taste of every thing. Nobody, human or animal, seemed happy.

Except Leslie. She was crazy about fixing up that broken-down old wreck of a house. She loved being needed by her father. Half the time they were supposed to be working they were just yakking away. She was learning, she related glowingly at recess, to "understand" her father. It had never occurred to Jess that parents were meant to be understood any more than the safe at the Millsburg First National was sitting around begging him to crack it. Parents were what they were; it wasn't up to you to try to puzzle them out. There was something weird about a grown man wanting to be friends with his own child. He ought to have friends his own age and let her have hers.

Jess's feelings about Leslie's father poked up like a canker sore. You keep biting it, and it gets bigger and worse instead of better. You spend a lot of time trying to keep your teeth away from it. Then sure as Christmas you forget the silly thing and chomp right down on it. Lord, that man got in his way. It even poisoned what time he did have with Leslie. She'd be sitting there bubbling away at recess, and it would be almost like the old times; then without warning, she'd say, "Bill thinks so and so." Chomp. Right down on the old sore.

Finally, finally she noticed. It took her until February, and for a girl as smart as Leslie that was a long, long time.

"Why don't you like Bill?"

"Who said I didn't?"

"Jess Aarons. How stupid do you think I am?"

Pretty stupid—sometimes. But what he actually said was, "What makes you think I don't like him?"

"Well, you never come to the house any more. At first I thought it was something I'd done. But it's not that. You still talk to me at school. Lots of times I see you in the field, playing with P. T., but you don't even come near the door."

"You're always busy." He was uncomfortably aware of how much he sounded like Brenda when he said this.

"Well, for spaghetti sauce! You could offer to help, you know."

It was like all the lights coming back on after an electrical storm. Lord, who was the stupid one?

Still, it took him a few days to feel comfortable around Leslie's father. Part of the problem was he didn't know what to call him. "Hey," he'd say, and both Leslie and her father would turn around. "Uh, Mr. Burke?"

"I wish you'd call me Bill, Jess."

"Yeah." He fumbled around with the name for a couple more days, but it came more easily with practice. It also helped to know some things that Bill for all his brains and books didn't know. Jess found he was really useful to him, not a nuisance to be tolerated or set out on the porch like P. T.

"You're amazing," Bill would say. "Where did you learn that, Jess?" Jess never quite knew how he knew things, so he'd shrug and let Bill and Leslie praise him to each other—though the work itself was praise enough.

First they ripped out the boards that covered the ancient fireplace, coming upon the rusty bricks like prospectors upon the mother lode. Next they got the old wallpaper off the living-room wall—all five garish layers of it. Sometimes as they lovingly patched and painted, they listened to Bill's records or sang, Leslie and Jess teaching Bill some of Miss Edmunds' songs and Bill teaching them some he knew. At other times they would talk. Jess listened wonderingly as Bill explained things that were going on in the world. If Momma could hear him, she'd swear he was another Walter Cronkite instead of "some hippie." All the Burkes were smart Not smart, maybe, about fixing things or growing things, but smart in a way Jess had never known real live people to be. Like one day while they were working, Judy came down and read out loud to them, mostly poetry and some of it in Italian which, of course, Jess couldn't understand, but he buried his head in the rich sound of the words and let himself be wrapped warmly around in the feel of the Burkes' brilliance.

They painted the living room gold. Leslie and Jess had wanted blue, but Bill held out for gold, which turned out to be so beautiful that they were glad they had given in. The sun would slant in from the west in the late afternoon until the room was brimful of light.

Finally Bill rented a sander from Millsburg Plaza, and they took off the black floor paint down to the wide oak boards and refinished them.

"No rugs," Bill said.

"No," agreed Judy. "It would be like putting a veil on the Mona Lisa."

When Bill and the children had finished razor-blading the last bits of paint off the windows and washed the panes, they called Judy down from her upstairs study to come and see. The four of them sat down on the floor and gazed around. It was gorgeous.

Leslie gave a deep satisfied sigh. "I love this room," she said. "Don't you feel the golden enchantment of it? It is worthy to be"—Jess looked up in sudden alarm—"in a palace." Relief. In such a mood, a person might even let a sworn secret slip. But she hadn't, not even to Bill and Judy, and he knew how she felt about her parents. She must have seen his anxiety because she winked at him across Bill and Judy just as he sometimes winked at May Belle over Joyce Ann's head. Terabithia was still just for the two of them.

The next afternoon they called P. T. and headed for Terabithia. It had been more than a month since they had been there together, and as they neared the creek bed, they slowed down. Jess wasn't sure he still remembered how to be a king.

"We've been away for many years," Leslie was whispering. "How do you suppose the kingdom has fared in our absence?"

"Where've we been?"

"Conquering the hostile savages on our northern borders," she answered. "But the lines of communication have been broken, and thus we do not have tidings of our beloved homeland for many a full moon." How was that for regular queen talk? Jess wished he could match it. "You think anything bad has happened?"

"We must have courage, my king. It may indeed be so."

They swung silently across the creek bed. On the farther bank, Leslie picked up two sticks. "Thy sword, sire," she whispered.

Jess nodded. They hunched down and crept toward the stronghold like police detectives on TV.

"Hey, queen! Watch out! Behind you!"

Leslie whirled and began to duel the imaginary foe. Then more came rushing upon them and the shouts of the battle rang through Terabithia. The guardian of the realm raced about in happy puppy circles, too young as yet to comprehend the danger that surrounded them all.

"They have sounded the retreat!" the brave queen cried.

"Yey!"

"Drive them out utterly, so they may never return and prey upon our people."

"Out you go! Out! Out!" All the way to the creek bed, they forced the enemy back, sweating under their winter jackets.

"At last, Terabithia is free once more."

The king sat down on a log and wiped his face, but the queen did not let him rest long. "Sire, we must go at once to the grove of the pines and give thanks for our victory."

Jess followed her into the grove, where they stood silently in the dim light.

"Who do we thank?" he whispered.

The question flickered across her face. "O God," she began. She was more at home with magic than religion. "O Spirits of the Grove."

"Thy right arm hast given us the victory." He couldn't remember where he'd heard that one, but it seemed to fit. Leslie gave him a look of approval.

She took up the words. "Now grant protection to Terabithia, to all its people, and to us its rulers."

"*Aroooo.*"

Jess tried hard not to smile. "And to its puppy dog."

"And to Prince Terrien, its guardian and jester. Amen."

"Amen."

They both managed somehow to keep the giggles buttoned in until they got out of the sacred place.

꙳

A few days after the encounter with the enemies of Terabithia, they had an encounter of a different sort at school. Leslie came out at recess to tell Jess that she had started into the girls' room only to be stopped by the sound of crying from one of the stalls. She lowered her voice. "This sounds crazy," she said. "But from the feet, I'm sure it's Janice Avery in there."

"You're kidding." The picture of Janice Avery crying on the toilet seat was too much for Jess to imagine.

"Well, she's the only one in school that has Willard Hughes's name crossed out on her sneakers. Besides, the smoke is so thick in there you need a gas mask."

"Are you sure she was crying?"

"Jess Aarons, I can tell if somebody's crying or not."

Lord, what was the matter with him? Janice Avery had given him nothing but trouble, and now he was feeling responsible for her—like one of the Burkes' timber wolves or beached whales. "She didn't even cry when kids teased her 'bout Willard after the note."

"Yeah. I know."

He looked at her. "Well," he said. "What should we do?"

"Do?" she asked. "What do you mean what should we do?"

How could he explain it to her? "Leslie. If she was an *animal* predator, we'd be obliged to try to help her."

Leslie gave him a funny look.

"Well, you're the one who's always telling me I gotta care," he said.

"But Janice Avery?"

"If she's crying, there gotta be something really wrong."

"Well, what are you planning to do?"

He flushed. "I can't go into no girls' room."

"Oh, I get it. You're going to send me into the shark's jaws. No, thank you, Mr. Aarons."

"Leslie, I swear—I'd go in there if I could." He really thought he would, too. "You ain't scared of her, are you, Leslie?" He didn't mean it in a daring way, he was just dumbfounded by the idea of Leslie being scared.

She flashed her eyes at him and tossed her head back in that proud way she had. "OK, I'm going in. But I want you to know, Jess Aarons, I think it's the dumbest idea you ever had in your life."

He crept down the hall after her and hid behind the nearest alcove to the girls' room door. He ought at least to be there to catch her when Janice kicked her out.

There was a quiet minute after the door swung shut behind Leslie. Then he heard Leslie saying something to Janice. Next a string of cuss words which were too loud to be blurred by the closed door. This was followed by some loud sobbing, not Leslie's, thank the Lord, and some sobbing and talking mixed up and—the bell.

He couldn't be caught staring at the door of the girls' room, but how could he leave? He'd be deserting in the line of fire. The rush of kids into the building settled it. He let himself be caught up in the stream and made his way to the basement steps, his brains still swirling with the sounds of cussing and sobbing.

Back in the fifth-grade classroom, he kept his eye glued on

the door for Leslie. He half expected to see her come through flattened straight out like the coyote on *Road Runner*. But she came in smiling without so much as a black eye. She waltzed over to Mrs. Myers and whispered her excuse for being late, and Mrs. Myers beamed at her with what was becoming known as the "Leslie Burke special."

How was he supposed to find out what had happened? If he tried to pass a note, the other kids would read it. Leslie sat way up in the front corner nowhere near the waste basket or pencil sharpener, so there was no way he could pretend to be heading somewhere else and sneak a word with her. And she wasn't moving in his direction. That was for sure. She was sitting straight up in her seat, looking as pleased with herself as a motorcycle rider who's just made it over fourteen trucks.

Leslie smirked clear through the afternoon and right on to the bus where Janice Avery gave her a little crooked smile on the way to the back seat, and Leslie looked over at Jess as if to say, "See!" He was going crazy wanting to know. She even put him off after the bus pulled away, pointing her head at May Belle as if to say, "We shouldn't discuss it in front of the children."

Finally, finally in the safe darkness of the stronghold she told him.

"Do you know why she was crying?"

"How'm I supposed to know? Lord, Leslie, will you tell me? What in the heck was going on in there?"

"Janice Avery is a very unfortunate person. Do you realize that?"

"What was she crying about, for heaven's sake?"

"It's a very complicated situation. I can understand now why Janice has so many problems relating to people."

"Will you tell me what happened before I have a hernia?"

"Did you know her father beats her?"

"Lots of kids' fathers beat 'um." *Will you get on with it*?

"No, I mean really beats her. The kind of beatings they take people to jail for in Arlington." She shook her head in disbelief. "You can't imagine. . . ."

"Is that why she was crying? Just 'cause her father beats her?"

"Oh, no. She gets beaten up all the time. She wouldn't cry at school about that."

"Then what *was* she crying for?"

"Well—" Lord, Leslie was loving this. She'd string him out forever. "Well, today she was so mad at her father that she told her so-called friends Wilma and Bobby Sue about it."

"Yeah?"

"And those two—two—" She looked for a word vile enough to describe Janice Avery's friends and found none. "Those two girls blabbed it all over the seventh grade."

Pity for Janice Avery swept across him.

"Even the teacher knows about it."

"Boy." The word came out like a sigh. There was a rule at Lark Creek, more important than anything Mr. Turner made up and fussed about. That was the rule that you never mixed up troubles at home with life at school. When parents were poor or ignorant or mean, or even just didn't believe in having a TV set, it was up to their kids to protect them. By tomorrow every kid and teacher in Lark Creek Elementary would be talking in half snickers about Janice Avery's daddy. It didn't matter if their own fathers were in the state hospital or the federal prison, they hadn't betrayed theirs, and Janice had.

"Do you know what else?"

"What?"

"I told Janice about not having a TV and everyone laughing.

I told her I understood what it was like to have everyone think I was weird."

"What'd she say to that?"

"She knew I was telling the truth. She even asked me for advice as if I was Dear Abby."

"Yeah?"

"I told her just to pretend she didn't know what on earth Wilma and Bobby Sue had said or where they had got such a crazy story and everybody would forget about it in a week." She leaned forward, suddenly anxious. "Do you think that was good advice?"

"Lord, how should I know? Make her feel better?"

"I think so. She seemed to feel a lot better."

"Well, it was great advice then."

She leaned back, happy and relaxed. "Know what, Jess?"

"What?"

"Thanks to you, I think I now have one and one-half friends at Lark Creek School."

It hurt him for it to mean so much to Leslie to have friends. When would she learn they weren't worth her trouble? "Oh, you got more friends than that."

"Nope. One and one-half. Monster Mouth Myers doesn't count."

There in their secret place, his feelings bubbled inside him like a stew on the back of the stove—some sad for her in her lonesomeness, but chunks of happiness, too. To be able to be Leslie's one whole friend in the world as she was his—he couldn't help being satisfied about that.

That night as he started to get into bed, leaving the light off so as not to wake the little girls, he was surprised by May Belle's shrill little "Jess."

"How come you still awake?"

"Jess. I know where you and Leslie go to hide."

"What d'you mean?"

"I followed ya."

He was at her bedside in one leap. "You ain't supposed to follow me!"

"How come?" Her voice was sassy.

He grabbed her shoulders and made her look him in the face. She blinked in the dim light like a startled chicken.

"You listen here, May Belle Aarons," he whispered fiercely, "I catch you following me again, your life ain't worth nothing."

"OK, OK."—she slid back into the bed—"Boy, you're mean. I oughta tell Momma on you."

"Look, May Belle, you can't do that. You can't tell Momma 'bout where me and Leslie go."

She answered with a little sniffing sound.

He grabbed her shoulders again. He was desperate. "I mean it, May Belle. You can't tell nobody nothing!" He let her go. "Now, I don't want to hear about you following me *or* squealing to Momma ever again, you hear?"

"Why not?"

" 'Cause if you do—I'm gonna tell Dilly Jean Edwards you still wet the bed sometimes."

"You wouldn't!"

"Boy, girl, you just better not try me."

He made her swear on the Bible never to tell and never to follow, but still he lay awake a long time. How could he trust everything that mattered to him to a sassy six-year-old? Sometimes it seemed to him that his life was delicate as a dandelion. One little puff from any direction, and it was blown to bits.

EIGHT

Easter

Even though it was nearly Easter, there were still very few nights that it was warm enough to leave Miss Bessie out. And then there was the rain. All March it poured. For the first time in many years the creek bed held water, not just a trickle either, enough so that when they swung across, it was a little scary looking down at the rushing water below. Jess took Prince Terrien across inside his jacket, but the puppy was growing so fast he might pop the zipper any time and fall into the water and drown.

Ellie and Brenda were already fighting about what they were going to wear to church. Since Momma got mad at the preacher three years back, Easter was the only time in the year that the Aarons went to church and it was a big deal. His mother always cried poor, but she put a lot of thought and as much money as she could scrape together into making sure she wouldn't be embarrassed by how her family looked. But the day before she planned to take them all over to Millsburg Plaza for new clothes, his dad came home from Washington early. He'd been laid off. No new clothes this year.

A wail went up from Ellie and Brenda like two sirens going to a fire. "You can't make me go to church," Brenda said. "I ain't got nothing to wear, and you know it."

"Just 'cause you're too fat," May Belle muttered.

"Did you hear what she said, Momma? I'm gonna kill that kid."

"Brenda, will you shut your mouth?" his mother said sharply; then more wearily, "We got lot more than Easter clothes to worry about."

His dad got up noisily and poured himself a cup of black coffee from the pot on the back of the stove.

"Why can't we charge some things?" Ellie said in her wheedling voice.

Brenda burst in. "Do you know what some people do? They charge something and wear it, and then take it back and say it didn't fit or something. The stores don't give 'em no trouble."

Her father turned in a kind of roar. "I never heard such a fool thing in my life. Didn't you hear your mother tell you to shut your mouth, girl!"

Brenda stopped talking, but she popped her gum as loudly as she could just to prove she wasn't going to be put down.

Jess was glad to escape to the shed and the complacent company of Miss Bessie. There was a knock. "Jess?"

"Leslie. Come on in."

She looked first and then sat on the floor near his stool. "What's new?"

"Lord, don't ask." He tugged the teats rhythmically and listened to the *plink, plink, plink*, in the bottom of the pail.

"That bad, huh?"

"My dad's got laid off, and Brenda and Ellie are fit to fry 'cause they can't have new clothes for Easter."

"Gee, I'm sorry. About your dad, I mean."

Jess grinned. "Yeah. I ain't too worried about those girls. If I know them, they'll trick new clothes out of somebody. It would make you throw up to see how those girls make a spectacle of themselves in church."

"I never knew you went to church."

"Just Easter." He concentrated on the warm udders. "I guess you think that's dumb or something."

She didn't answer for a minute. "I was thinking I'd like to go."

He stopped milking. "I don't understand you sometimes, Leslie."

"Well, I've never been to a church before. It would be a new experience for me."

He went back to work. "You'd hate it."

"Why?"

"It's boring."

"Well, I'd just like to see for myself. Do you think your parents would let me go with you?"

"You can't wear pants."

"I've got some dresses, Jess Aarons." Would wonders never cease?

"Here," he said. "Open your mouth."

"Why?"

"Just open your mouth." For once she obeyed. He sent a stream of warm milk straight into it.

"Jess Aarons!" The name was garbled and the milk dribbled down her chin as she spoke.

"Don't open your mouth now. You're wasting good milk."

Leslie started to giggle, choking and coughing.

"Now if I could just learn to pitch a baseball that straight. Lemme try again."

Leslie controlled her giggle, closed her eyes, and solemnly opened her mouth.

But now Jess was giggling, so that he couldn't keep his hand steady.

"You dunce! You got me right in the ear." Leslie hunched up her shoulder and rubbed her ear with the sleeve of her sweat shirt. She collapsed into giggles again.

"I'd be obliged if you'd finish milking and come on back to the house." His dad was standing right there at the door.

"I guess I'd better go," said Leslie quietly. She got up and went to the door. "Excuse me." His dad moved aside to let her pass. Jess waited for him to say something more, but he just stood there for a few minutes and then turned and went out.

Ellie said she would go to church if Momma would let her wear the see-through blouse, and Brenda would go if she at least got a new skirt. In the end everyone got something new except Jess and his dad, neither of whom cared, but Jess got the idea it might give him a little bargaining power with his mother.

"Since I ain't getting anything new, could Leslie go to church with us?"

"That girl?" He could see his mother rooting around in her head for a good reason to say no. "She don't dress right."

"Momma!"—his voice sounded as prissy as Ellie's—"Leslie's got dresses. She got hundreds of 'um."

His mother's thin face drooped. She bit the outside of her bottom lip in a way Joyce Ann sometimes did and spoke so softly Jess could hardly hear her. "I don't want no one poking up their nose at my family."

Jess wanted to put his arm around her the way he put it around May Belle when she was in need of comfort. "She don't poke her nose up at you, Momma. Honest."

His mother sighed. "Well, if she'll look decent. . . ."

Leslie looked decent. Her hair was kind of slicked down, and she wore a navy-blue jumper over a blouse with tiny old-fashioned-looking flowers. At the bottom of her red knee socks were a pair of shiny brown leather shoes that Jess had never seen before as Leslie always wore sneakers like the rest of the kids in Lark Creek. Even her manner was decent. Her usual sparkle was toned way down, and she said "Yes'm" and "No'm" to his mother just as though she were aware of Mrs. Aaron's dread of disrespect. Jess knew how hard Leslie must be trying, for Leslie didn't say "ma'am" naturally.

In comparison to Leslie, Brenda and Ellie looked like a

pair of peacocks with fake tail feathers. They both insisted on riding in the front of the pickup with their parents, which was some kind of a squeeze with Brenda's shape to consider. Jess and Leslie and the little girls climbed happily into the back and sat down on the old sacks his dad had put against the cab.

The sun wasn't exactly shining, but it was the first day in so long that the rain wasn't actually coming down that they sang "O Lord, What a Morning," "Ah, Lovely Meadows," and "Sing! Sing a Song" that Miss Edmunds had taught them, and even "Jingle Bells" for Joyce Ann. The wind carried their voices away from them. It made the music seem mysterious, which filled Jess with a feeling of power over the hills rolling out from behind the truck. The ride was much too short, especially for Joyce Ann, who began to cry because the arrival interrupted the first verse of "Santa Claus Is Coming to Town," which after "Jingle Bells" was her favorite song. Jess tickled her to get her giggling again, so that when the four of them clambered down over the tail gate, they were flushed-faced and happy once more.

They were a little late, which didn't bother Ellie and Brenda for it meant that they got to flounce down the entire length of the aisle to the first pew, making sure that every eye in the church was on them, and every expression of every eye a jealous one. Lord, they were disgusting. And his mother had been scared Leslie might embarrass her. Jess hunched his shoulders and slunk into the pew after the string of women-folks and just before his dad.

Church always seemed the same. Jess could tune it out the same way he tuned out school, with his body standing up and sitting down in unison with the rest of the congregation but his mind numb and floating, not really thinking or dreaming but at least free.

Once or twice he was aware of being on his feet with the loud not really tuneful singing all around him. At the edge of his consciousness he could hear Leslie singing along and drowsily wondered why she bothered.

The preacher had one of those tricky voices. It would buzz along for several minutes quite comfortably, then bang! he was screaming at you. Each time Jess would jump, and it would take another couple of minutes to relax again. Because he wasn't listening to the words, the man's red face with sweat pouring down seemed strangely out of place in the dull sanctuary. It was like Brenda throwing a tantrum over Joyce Ann touching her lipstick.

It took a while to get Ellie and Brenda pulled away from the front yard of the church. Jess and Leslie went ahead and put the little girls in the back and settled down to wait.

"Gee, I'm really glad I came."

Jess turned to Leslie in unbelief.

"It was better than a movie."

"You're kidding."

"No, I'm not." And she wasn't. He could tell by her face. "That whole Jesus thing is really interesting, isn't it?"

"What d'you mean?"

"All those people wanting to kill him when he hadn't done anything to hurt them." She hesitated. "It's really kind of a beautiful story—like Abraham Lincoln or Socrates—or Aslan."

"It ain't beautiful," May Belle broke in. "It's scary. Nailing holes right through somebody's hand."

"May Belle's right." Jess reached down into the deepest pit of his mind. "It's because we're all vile sinners God made Jesus die."

"Do you think that's true?"

He was shocked. "It's in the Bible, Leslie."

She looked at him as if she were going to argue, then seemed to change her mind. "It's crazy, isn't it?" She shook her head. "You have to believe it, but you hate it. I don't have to believe it, and I think it's beautiful." She shook her head again. "It's crazy."

May Belle had her eyes all squinched as though Leslie was some strange creature in a zoo. "You gotta believe the Bible, Leslie."

"Why?" It was a genuine question. Leslie wasn't being smarty.

" 'Cause if you don't believe the Bible"—May Belle's eyes were huge—"God'll damn you to hell when you die."

"Where'd she ever hear a thing like that?" Leslie turned on Jess as though she were about to accuse him of some wrong he had committed against his sister. He felt hot and caught by her voice and words.

He dropped his gaze to the gunnysack and began to fiddle with the raveled edge.

"That's right, ain't it, Jess?" May Belle's shrill voice demanded, "Don't God damn you to hell if you don't believe the Bible?

Jess pushed his hair out of his face. "I reckon," he muttered.

"I don't believe it," Leslie said. "I don't even think you've read the Bible."

"I read most of it." Jess said, still fingering the sack. "S'bout the only book we got around our place." He looked up at Leslie and half grinned.

She smiled. "OK," she said. "But I still don't think God goes around damning people to hell."

They smiled at each other trying to ignore May Belle's anxious little voice. "But Leslie," she insisted. "What if you *die*? What's going to happen to you if you *die*?"

The Evil Spell

On Easter Monday the rain began again in earnest. It was as though the elements were conspiring to ruin their short week of freedom. Jess and Leslie sat cross-legged on the porch at the Burkes', watching the wheels of a passing truck shoot huge sprays of muddy water to its rear.

"That ain't no fifty-five miles per hour," Jess muttered.

Just then something came out of the window of the cab. Leslie jumped to her feet. "Litterbug!" she screamed after the already disappearing taillights.

Jess stood up, too. "What d'ya want to do?"

"What I want to do is go to Terabithia," she said, looking out mournfully at the pouring rain.

"Heck, let's go," he said.

"OK," she said, suddenly brightening. "Why not?"

She got her boots and raincoat and considered the umbrella. "D'ya think we could swing across holding the umbrella?"

He shook his head. "Nah."

"We better stop by your house and get your boots and things."

He shrugged. "I don't have nothing that fits. I'll just go like this."

"I'll get you an old coat of Bill's." She started up the stairs. Judy appeared in the hallway.

"What are you kids doing?" It was the same words that Jess's mother might have used, but it didn't come out the same way. Judy's eyes were kind of fuzzed over as she spoke, and her voice sounded as though it were being broadcast from miles away.

"We didn't mean to bother you, Judy."

"That's all right, I'm stuck right now. I might as well stop. Have you had any lunch?"

"S'all right, Judy. We can get something ourselves."

Judy's eyes focused slightly. "You've got your boots on."

Leslie looked down at her feet. "Oh, yeah," she said, as though she were just noticing them herself. "We thought we'd go out for a while."

"Is it raining again?"

"Yeah."

"I used to like to walk in the rain." Judy smiled the kind of smile May Belle did in her sleep. "Well, if you two can manage. . . ."

"Sure."

"Is Bill back yet?"

"No. He said he wouldn't be back until late, not to worry."

"Fine," she said. "Oh," she said suddenly, and her eyes popped wide open. "Oh!" She almost ran back to her room, and the plinkety-plink of the typewriter began at once.

Leslie was grinning. "She came unstuck."

He wondered what it would be like to have a mother whose stories were inside her head instead of marching across the television screen all day long. He followed Leslie up the hall to where she was pulling things out of a closet. She handed him a beige raincoat and a peculiar round black woolly hat.

"No boots." Her voice was coming out of the depths of the closet and was muffled by a line of overcoats. "How about a pair of clumps?"

"A pair of what?"

She stuck her head out between the coats. "Cleats. Cleats." She produced them. They looked like size twelves.

"Naw. I'd lose 'em in the mud. I'll just go barefoot."

"Hey," she said, emerging completely. "Me, too."

The ground was cold. The icy mud sent little thrills of pain up their legs, so they ran, splashing through the puddles and slushing in the mud. P. T. bounded ahead, leaping fishlike from one brown sea to the next, then turning back to herd the two of them forward, nipping at their heels and further splashing their already sopping jeans.

When they got to the bank of the creek, they stopped. It was an awesome sight. Like in *The Ten Commandments* on TV when the water came rushing into the dry path Moses had made and swept all the Egyptians away, the long dry bed of the creek was a roaring eight-foot-wide sea, sweeping before it great branches of trees, logs, and trash, swirling them about like so many Egyptian chariots, the hungry waters licking and sometimes leaping the banks, daring them to try to confine it.

"Wow." Leslie's voice was respectful.

"Yeah." Jess looked up at the rope. It was still twisted around the branch of the crab apple tree. His stomach felt cold. "Maybe we ought to forget it today."

"C'mon, Jess. We can make it." The hood of Leslie's rain-

coat had fallen back, and her hair lay plastered to her forehead. She wiped her cheeks and eyes with her hand and then
untwisted the rope. She unsnapped the top of her coat with her
left hand. "Here," she said. "Stick P. T. in here for me."

"I'll carry him, Leslie."

"With that raincoat, he'll slip right out the bottom." She
was impatient to be gone, so Jess scooped up the sodden dog,
and shoved him rear-first into the cave of Leslie's raincoat.

"You gotta hold his rear with your left arm and swing with
your right, you know."

"I know. I know." She moved backward to get a running
start.

"Hold tight."

"Good gosh, Jess."

He shut his mouth. He wanted to shut his eyes, too. But he
forced himself to watch her run back, race for the bank, leap,
swing, and jump off, landing gracefully on her feet on the far
side.

"Catch!"

He stuck his hand out, but he was watching Leslie and P.
T. and not concentrating on the rope, which slipped off the
end of his fingertips and swung in a large arc out of his reach.
He jumped and grabbed it, and shutting his mind to the sound
and sight of the water, he ran back and then speeded forward.
The cold stream lapped his bare heels momentarily, but then
he was into the air above it and falling awkwardly and landing on his bottom. P. T. was on him immediately, muddy paws
all over the beige raincoat, and pink tongue sandpapering
Jess's wet face.

Leslie's eyes were sparkling. "Arise"—she barely swallowed a giggle—"arise, king of Terabithia, and let us proceed
into our kingdom."

The king of Terabithia snuffled and wiped his face on the

back of his hand. "I will arise," he replied with dignity, "when thou removes this fool dog off my gut."

They went to Terabithia on Tuesday and again on Wednesday. The rain continued sporadically, so that by Wednesday the creek had swollen to the trunk of the crab apple and they were runing through ankle-deep water to make their flight into Terabithia. And on the opposite bank Jess was more careful to land on his feet. Sitting in cold wet britches for an hour was no fun even in a magic kingdom.

For Jess the fear of the crossing rose with the height of the creek. Leslie never seemed to hesitate, so Jess could not hang back. But even though he could force his body to follow after, his mind hung back, wanting to cling to the crab apple tree the way Joyce Ann might cling to Momma's skirt.

While they were sitting in the castle on Wednesday, it began suddenly to rain so hard that water came through the top of the shack in icy streams. Jess tried to huddle away from the worst of them, but there was no escaping the miserable invaders.

"Dost know what is in my mind, O king?" Leslie dumped the contents of one coffee can on the ground and put the can under the worst leak.

"What?"

"Methinks some evil being has put a curse on our beloved kingdom."

"Damn weather bureau." In the dim light he could see Leslie's face freeze into its most queenly pose—the kind of expression she usually reserved for vanquished enemies. She didn't want to kid. He instantly repented his unkingly manner.

Leslie chose to ignore it. "Let us go even up into the sacred grove and inquire of the Spirits what this evil might be and how we must combat it. For of a truth I perceive that this is no ordinary rain that is falling upon our kingdom."

"Right, queen," Jess mumbled and crawled out of the low entrance of the castle stronghold.

Under the pines even the rain lost its driving power. Without the filtered light of the sun it was almost dark, and the sound of the rain hitting the pine branches high above their heads filled the grove with a weird, tuneless music. Dread lay on Jess's stomach like a hunk of cold, undigested doughnut.

Leslie lifted her arms and face up toward the dark green canopy. "O Spirits of the grove," she began solemnly. "We are come on behalf of our beloved kingdom which lies even now under the spell of some evil, unknown force. Give us, we beseech thee, wisdom to discern this evil, and power to overcome it." She nudged Jess with her elbow.

He raised his arms. "Um. Uh." He felt the point of her sharp elbow again. "Um. Yes. Please listen, thou Spirits."

She seemed satisfied. At least she didn't poke him again. She just stood there quietly as if she was listening respectfully to someone talking to her. Jess was shivering, whether from the cold or the place, he didn't know. But he was glad when she turned to leave the grove. All he could think of was dry clothes and a cup of hot coffee and maybe just plunking down in front of the TV for a couple of hours. He was obviously not worthy to be king of Terabithia. Whoever heard of a king who was scared of tall trees and a little bit of water?

He swung across the creek almost too disgusted with himself to be afraid. Halfway across he looked down and stuck his tongue out at the roaring below. *Who's afraid of the big bad wolf? Tra-la-la-la-la,* he said to himself, then quickly looked up again toward the crab apple tree.

Plodding up the hill through the mud and beaten-down grasses, he slammed his bare feet down hard. *Left, left,* he

addressed them inside his head. *Left my wife and forty-nine children without any gingerbread, think I did right? Right. Right by my* . . .

"Why don't we change our clothes and watch TV or something over at your house?"

He felt like hugging her. "I'll make us some coffee," he said joyfully.

"Yuk," she said smiling and began to run for the old Perkins place, that beautiful, graceful run of hers that neither mud nor water could defeat.

🌿

It had seemed to Jess when he went to bed Wednesday night that he could relax, that everything was going to be all right, but he awoke in the middle of the night with the horrible realization that it was still raining. He would just have to tell Leslie that he wouldn't go to Terabithia. After all, she had told him that when she was working on the house with Bill. And he hadn't questioned her. It wasn't so much that he minded telling Leslie that he was afraid to go; it was that he minded being afraid. It was as though he had been made with a great piece missing—one of May Belle's puzzles with this huge gap where somebody's eye and cheek and jaw should have been. Lord, it would be better to be born without an arm than to go through life with no guts. He hardly slept the rest of the night, listening to the horrid rain and knowing that no matter how high the creek came, Leslie would still want to cross it.

TEN

The Perfect Day

He heard his dad start the pickup. Even though there was no job to go to, he left every morning early to look. Sometimes he just hung around all day at the unemployment office; on lucky days he got picked up to unload furniture or do cleaning.

Jess was awake. He might as well get up. He could milk and feed Miss Bessie, and get that over with. He pulled on a T-shirt and overalls over the underwear he slept in.

"Where you going?"

"Go back to sleep, May Belle."

"I can't. The rain makes too much noise."

"Well, get up then."

"Why are you so mean to me?"

"Will you shut up, May Belle? You'll have everyone in the whole house woke up with that big mouth of yours."

Joyce Ann would have screamed, but May Belle made a face.

"Oh, c'mon," he said. "I'm just gonna milk Miss Bessie. Then maybe we can watch cartoons if we keep the sound real low."

May Belle was as scrawny as Brenda was fat. She stood a moment in the middle of the floor in her underwear, her skin white and goose-bumpy. Her eyes were still drooped from sleep, and her pale brown hair stuck up all over her head like a squirrel's nest on a winter branch. That's got to be the world's ugliest kid, he thought, looking her over with genuine affection.

She threw her jeans into his face. "I'm gonna tell Momma."

He threw the jeans back at her. "Tell Momma what?"

"How you just stand there staring at me when I ain't got my clothes on."

Lord. She thought he was enjoying it. "Yeah, well," he said, heading for the door so she wouldn't throw anything else at him. "Pretty girl like you. Can't hardly help myself." He could hear her giggling as he crossed the kitchen.

The shed was filled with Miss Bessie's familiar smell. He clucked her gently over and set his stool at her flank and the pail beneath her speckled udder. The rain pounded the metal roof of the shed so that the plink of milk in the pail set up a counter-rhythm. If only it would stop raining. He pressed his forehead against Miss Bessie's warm hide. He wondered idly if cows were ever scared—really scared. He had seen Miss Bessie jitter away from P.T., but that was different. A yapping puppy at your heels is an immediate threat, but the difference between him and Miss Bessie was that when there was no P. T. in sight she was perfectly content, sleepily chewing her cud. She wasn't staring down at the old Perkins place, wondering and worrying. She wasn't standing there on her tippytoes while anxiety ate holes through all her stomachs.

He stroked his forehead across her flank and sighed. If there was still water in the creek come summer, he'd ask Leslie to teach him how to swim. How's that? he said to himself. I'll just grab that old terror by the shoulders and shake the daylights out of it. Maybe I'll even learn scuba diving. He shuddered. He may not have been born with guts, but he didn't have to die without them. Hey, maybe you could go down to the Medical College and get a gut transplant. No, Doc, I got me a perfectly good heart. What I need is a *gut* transplant. How 'bout it? He smiled. He'd have to tell Leslie about wanting a gut transplant. It was the kind of nonsense she appreciated. Of course—he broke the rhythm of the milking long enough to shove his hair out of his face—of course what I really need is a brain transplant. I know Leslie. I know she's not going to bite my head off or make fun of me if I say I don't want to go across again till the creek's down. All I gotta do is say "Leslie, I don't wanta go over there today." Just like that. Easy as pie. "Leslie, I don't want to go over there today." "How come?" "How come. Because, because, well because. . . ."

"I called ya three times already." May Belle was imitating Ellie's prissiest manner.

"Called me for what?"

"Some lady wants you on the telephone. I had to get dressed to come get you."

He never got phone calls. Leslie had called him exactly once, and Brenda had gone into such a song and dance with her about Jess's getting a call from his *sweetheart* that Leslie had decided it was simpler to come to the house and get him when she wanted to talk.

"Sounds kinda like Miss Edmunds."

It was Miss Edmunds. "Jess?" her voice flowed through the receiver. "Miserable weather, isn't it?"

"Yes'm." He was scared to say more for fear she'd hear the shake.

"I was thinking of driving down to Washington—maybe go to the Smithsonian or the National Gallery. How would you like to keep me company?"

He broke out in a cold sweat.

"Jess?"

He licked his lips and shoved his hair off his face.

"You still there, Jess?"

"Yes'm." He tried to get a deep breath so he could keep talking.

"Would you like to go with me?"

Lord. "Yes'm."

"Do you need to get permission?" she asked gently.

"Yes—yes'm." He had somehow managed to twist himself up in the phone cord. "Yes'm. Just—just a minute." He untangled himself, put the phone down quietly, and tiptoed into his parents' room. His mother's back made a long hump under the cotton blanket. He shook her shoulder very gently. "Momma?" he was almost whispering. He wanted to ask her without really waking her up. She was likely to say no if she woke up and thought about it.

She jumped at the sound but relaxed again, not fully awake.

"Teacher wants me to go to Washington to the Smithsonian."

"Washington?" The syllables were blurred.

"Yeah. Something for school." He stroked her upper arm. "Be back before too late. OK?"

"Umm."

"Don't worry. I done milking."

"Umm." She pulled the blanket to her ears and turned on her stomach.

Jess crept back to the phone. "It's OK, Miss Edmunds. I can go."

"Great. I'll pick you up in twenty minutes. Just tell me how to get to your house."

As soon as he saw her car turn in, Jess raced out the kitchen door through the rain and met her halfway up the drive. His mother could find out the details from May Belle after he was safely up the road. He was glad May Belle was absorbed in the TV. He didn't want her waking Momma up before he got away. He was scared to look back even after he was in the car and on the main road for fear he'd see his mother screaming after him.

It didn't occur to him until the car was past Millsburg that he might have asked Miss Edmunds if Leslie could have come, too. When he thought about it, he couldn't suppress a secret pleasure at being alone in this small cozy car with Miss Edmunds. She drove intently, both hands gripping the top of the wheel, peering forward. The wheels hummed and the windshield wipers slicked a merry rhythm. The car was warm and filled with the smell of Miss Edmunds. Jess sat with his hands clasped between his knees, the seat belt tight across his chest.

"Damn rain," she said. "I was going stir crazy."

"Yes'm," he said happily.

"You, too, huh?" She gave him a quick smile.

He felt dizzy from the closeness. He nodded.

"Have you ever been to the National Gallery?"

"No, ma'am." He had never even been to Washington before, but he hoped she wouldn't ask him that.

She smiled at him again. "Is this your first trip to an art gallery?"

"Yes'm."

"Great," she said. "My life has been worthwhile after all." He didn't understand her, but he didn't care. He knew she was happpy to be with him, and that was enough to know.

Even in the rain he could make out the landmarks, looking surprisingly the way the books had pictured them—the Lee Mansion high on the hill, the bridge, and twice around the circle, so he could get a good look at Abraham Lincoln looking out across the city, the White House and the Monument and at the other end the Capitol. Leslie had seen all these places a million times. She had even gone to school with a girl whose father was a congressman. He thought he might tell Miss Edmunds later that Leslie was a personal friend of a real congressman. Miss Edmunds had always liked Leslie.

Entering the gallery was like stepping inside the pine grove —the huge vaulted marble, the cool splash of the fountain, and the green growing all around. Two little children had pulled away from their mothers and were running about, screaming to each other. It was all Jess could do not to grab them and tell them how to behave in so obviously a sacred place.

And then the pictures—room after room, floor after floor. He was drunk with color and form and hugeness—and with the voice and perfume of Miss Edmunds always beside him. She would bend her head down close to his face to give some explanation or ask him a question, her black hair falling across her shoulders. Men would stare at her instead of the pictures, and Jess felt they must be jealous of him for being with her.

They ate a late lunch in the cafeteria. When she mentioned lunch, he realized with horror that he would need money, and he didn't know how to tell her that he hadn't brought any— didn't have any to bring, for that matter. But before he had time to figure anything out, she said, "Now I'm not going to have any argument about whose paying. I'm a liberated woman, Jess Aarons. When I invite a man out, I pay."

He tried to think of some way to protest without ending up with the bill, but couldn't, and found himself getting a three-dollar meal, which was far more than he had meant to have her spend on him. Tomorrow he would check out with Leslie how he should have handled things.

After lunch, they trotted through the drizzle to the Smithsonian to see the dinosaurs and the Indians. There they came upon a display case holding a miniature scene of Indians disguised in buffalo skins scaring a herd of buffalo into stampeding over a cliff to their death with more Indians waiting below to butcher and skin them. It was a three-dimensional nightmare version of some of his own drawings. He felt a frightening sense of kinship with it.

"Fascinating, isn't it?" Miss Edmunds said, her hair brushing his cheek as she leaned over to look at it.

He touched his cheek. "Yes'm." To himself he said, *I don't think I like it*, but he could hardly pull himself away.

When they came out of the building, it was into brilliant

spring sunshine. Jess blinked his eyes against the glare and the glisten.

"Wow!" Miss Edmunds said. "A miracle! Behold the sun! I was beginning to think she had gone into a cave and vowed never to return, like the Japanese myth."

He felt good again. All the way home in the sunshine Miss Edmunds told funny stories about going to college one year in Japan, where all the boys had been shorter than she, and she hadn't known how to use the toilets.

He relaxed. He had so much to tell Leslie and ask her. It didn't matter how angry his mother was. She'd get over it. And it was worth it. This one perfect day of his life was worth anything he had to pay.

One dip in the road before the old Perkins place, he said, "Just let me out at the road, Miss Edmunds. Don't try to turn in. You might get stuck in the mud."

"OK, Jess," she said. She pulled over at his road. "Thank you for a beautiful day."

The western sun danced on the windshield dazzling his eyes. He turned and looked Miss Edmunds full in the face. "No, ma'am." His voice sounded squeaky and strange. He cleared his throat. "No ma'am, thank *you*. Well——" He hated to leave without being able to really thank her, but the words were not coming for him now. Later, of course, they would, when he was lying in bed or sitting in the castle. "Well——" He opened the door and got out. "See you next Friday."

She nodded, smiling. "See you."

He watched the car go out of sight and then turned and ran with all his might to the house, the joy jiggling inside of him so hard that he wouldn't have been surprised if his feet had just taken off from the ground the way they sometimes did in dreams and floated him right over the roof.

He was all the way into the kitchen before he realized that

something was wrong. His dad's pickup had been outside the door, but he hadn't taken it in until he came into the room and found them all sitting there: his parents and the little girls at the kitchen table and Ellie and Brenda on the couch. Not eating. There was no food on the table. Not watching TV. It wasn't even turned on. He stood unmoving for a second while they stared at him.

Suddenly his mother let out a great shuddering sob. "O my God. O my God." She said it over and over, her head down on her arms. His father moved to put his arm around her awkwardly, but he didn't take his eyes off Jess.

"I tolja he just gone off somewhere," May Belle said quietly and stubbornly as though she had repeated it often and no one had believed her.

He squinted his eyes as though trying to peer down a dark drain pipe. He didn't even know what question to ask them. "What—?" he tried to begin.

Brenda's pouting voice broke in, "Your girl friend's dead, and Momma thought you was dead, too."

No!

Something whirled around inside Jess's head. He opened his mouth, but it was dry and no words came out. He jerked his head from one face to the next for someone to help him.

Finally his father spoke, his big rough hand stroking his wife's hair and his eyes downcast watching the motion. "They found the Burke girl this morning down in the creek."

"No," he said, finding his voice. "Leslie wouldn't drown. She could swim real good."

"That old rope you kids been swinging on broke." His father went quietly and relentlessly on. "They think she musta hit her head on something when she fell."

"No." He shook his head. "No."

His father looked up. "I'm real sorry, boy."

"No!" Jess was yelling now. "I don't believe you. You're

lying to me!" He looked around again wildly for someone to agree. But they all had their heads down except May Belle, whose eyes were wide with terror. *But, Leslie, what if you die?*

"No," he said straight at May Belle. "It's a lie. Leslie ain't dead." He turned around and ran out the door, letting the screen bang sharply against the house. He ran down the gravel to the main road and then started running west away from Washington and Millsburg—and the old Perkins place. An approaching car beeped and swerved and beeped again, but he hardly noticed.

Leslie—dead—girl friend—rope—broke—fell—you—you —you. The words exploded in his head like corn against the sides of the popper. *God—dead—you—Leslie—dead—you.* He ran until he was stumbling but he kept on, afraid to stop. Knowing somehow that running was the only thing that could keep Leslie from being dead. It was up to him. He had to keep going.

Behind him came the *baripity* of the pickup, but he couldn't turn around. He tried to run faster, but his father passed him and stopped the pickup just ahead, then jumped out and ran back. He picked Jess up in his arms as though he were a baby. For the first few seconds Jess kicked and struggled against the strong arms. Then Jess gave himself over to the numbness that was buzzing to be let out from a corner of his brain.

He leaned his weight upon the door of the pickup and let his head thud-thud against the window. His father drove stiffly without speaking, though once he cleared his throat as though he were going to say something, but he glanced at Jess and closed his mouth.

When they pulled up at his house, his father sat quietly, and Jess could feel the man's uncertainty, so he opened the

door and got out, and with the numbness flooding through him, went in and lay down on his bed.

❦

He was awake, jerked suddenly into consciousness in the black stillness of the house. He sat up, stiff and shivering, although he was fully dressed from his windbreaker down to his sneakers. He could hear the breathing of the little girls in the next bed, strangely loud and uneven in the quiet. Some dream must have awakened him, but he could not remember it. He could only remember the mood of dread it had brought with it. Through the curtainless window he could see the lopsided moon with hundreds of stars dancing in bright attendance.

It came into his mind that someone had told him that Leslie was dead. But he knew now that that had been part of the dreadful dream. Leslie could not die any more than he himself could die. But the words turned over uneasily in his mind like leaves stirred up by a cold wind. If he got up now and went down to the old Perkins place and knocked on the door, Leslie would come to open it, P. T. jumping at her heels like a star around the moon. It was a beautiful night. Perhaps they could run over the hill and across the fields to the stream and swing themselves into Terabithia.

They had never been there in the dark. But there was enough moon for them to find their way into the castle, and he could tell her about his day in Washington. And apologize. It had been so dumb of him not to ask if Leslie could go, too. He and Leslie and Miss Edmunds could have had a wonderful day—different, of course, from the day he and Miss Edmunds had had, but still good, still perfect. Miss Edmunds and Leslie liked each other a lot. It would have been fun to have Leslie along. *I'm really sorry, Leslie.* He took off his jacket and sneakers, and crawled under the covers. *I was dumb not to think of asking.*

S'OK, Leslie would say. *I've been to Washington thousands of times.*

Did you ever see the buffalo hunt?

Somehow it was the one thing in all Washington that Leslie had never seen, and so he could tell her about it, describing the tiny beasts hurtling to destruction.

His stomach felt suddenly cold. It had something to do with the buffalo, with falling, with death. With the reason he had not remembered to ask if Leslie could go with them to Washington today.

You know something weird?

What? Leslie asked.

I was scared to come to Terabithia this morning.

The coldness threatened to spread up from his stomach. He turned over and lay on it. Perhaps it would be better not to think about Leslie right now. He would go to see her the first thing in the morning and explain everything. He could explain it better in the daytime when he had shaken off the effects of his unremembered nightmare.

He put his mind to remembering the day in Washington, working on details of pictures and statues, dredging up the sound of Miss Edmunds' voice, recalling his own exact words and her exact answers. Occasionally into the corner of his mind's vision would come a sensation of falling, but he pushed it away with the view of another picture or the sound of another conversation. Tomorrow he must share it all with Leslie.

The next thing he was aware of was the sun streaming through the window. The little girls' bed was only rumpled covers, and there was movement and quiet talking from the kitchen.

Lord! Poor Miss Bessie. He'd forgotten all about her last night, and now it must be late. He felt for his sneakers and shoved his feet over the heels without tying the laces.

His mother looked up quickly from the stove at the sound of him. Her face was set for a question, but she just nodded her head at him.

The coldness began to come back. "I forgot Miss Bessie."

"Your daddy's milking her."

"I forgot last night, too."

She kept nodding her head. "Your daddy did it for you." But it wasn't an accusation. "You feel like some breakfast?"

Maybe that was why his stomach felt so odd. He hadn't had anything to eat since the ice cream Miss Edmunds had bought them at Millsburg on the way home. Brenda and Ellie stared up at him from the table. The little girls turned from their cartoon show at the TV to look at him and then turned quickly back.

He sat down on the bench. His mother put a plateful of pancakes in front of him. He couldn't remember the last time she had made pancakes. He doused them with syrup and began to eat. They tasted marvelous.

"You don't even care. Do you?" Brenda was watching him from across the table.

He looked at her puzzled, his mouth full.

"If Jimmy Dicks died, I wouldn't be able to eat a bite."

The coldness curled up inside of him and flopped over.

"Will you shut your mouth, Brenda Aarons?" His mother sprang forward, the pancake turner held threateningly high.

"Well, Momma, he's just sitting there eating pancakes like nothing happened. I'd be crying my eyes out."

Ellie was looking first at Mrs. Aarons and then at Brenda. "Boys ain't supposed to cry at times like this. Are they, Momma?"

"Well, it don't seem right for him to be sitting there eating like a brood sow."

"I'm telling you, Brenda, if you don't shut your mouth. . . ."

He could hear them talking but they were farther away than the memory of the dream. He ate and he chewed and he swallowed, and when his mother put three more pancakes on his plate, he ate them, too.

His father came in with the milk. He poured it carefully into the empty cider jugs and put them into the refrigerator. Then he washed his hands at the sink and came to the table. As he passed Jess, he put his hand lightly on the boy's shoulder. He wasn't angry about the milking.

Jess was only dimly aware that his parents were looking at each other and then at him. Mrs. Aarons gave Brenda a hard look and gave Mr. Aarons a look which was to say that Brenda was to be kept quiet, but Jess was only thinking of how good the pancakes had been and hoping his mother would put down some more in front of him. He knew somehow that he shouldn't ask for more, but he was disappointed that she didn't give him any. He thought, then, that he should get up and leave the table, but he wasn't sure where he was supposed to go or what he was supposed to do.

"Your mother and I thought we ought to go down to the neighbors and pay respects." His father cleared his throat. "I think it would be fitting for you to come, too." He stopped again. "Seeing's you was the one that really knowed the little girl."

Jess tried to understand what his father was saying to him, but he felt stupid. "What little girl?" He mumbled it, knowing it was the wrong thing to ask. Ellie and Brenda both gasped.

His father leaned down the table and put his big hand on top of Jess's hand. He gave his wife a quick, troubled look. But she just stood there, her eyes full of pain, saying nothing.

"Your friend Leslie is dead, Jesse. You need to understand that."

Jess slid his hand out from under his father's. He got up from the table.

"I know it ain't a easy thing—" Jess could hear his father speaking as he went into the bedroom. He came back out with his windbreaker on.

"You ready to go now?" His father got up quickly. His mother took off her apron and patted her hair.

May Belle jumped up from the rug. "I wanta go, too," she said. "I never seen a dead person before."

"No!" May Belle sat down again as though slapped down by her mother's voice.

"We don't even know where she's laid out at, May Belle," Mr. Aarons said more gently.

Stranded

They walked slowly across the field and down the hill to the old Perkins place. There were four or five cars parked outside. His father raised the knocker. Jess could hear P. T. barking from the back of the house and rushing to the door.

"Hush, P. T.," a voice which Jess did not know said. "Down." The door was opened by a man who was half leaning over to hold the dog back. At the sight of Jess, P. T. snatched himself loose and leapt joyfully upon the boy. Jess picked him up and rubbed the back of the dog's neck as he used to when P. T. was a tiny puppy.

"I see he knows you," the strange man said with a funny half smile on his face. "Come in, won't you." He stood back for the three of them to enter.

They went into the golden room, and it was just the same, except more beautiful because the sun was pouring through the south windows. Four or five people Jess had never seen before were sitting about, whispering some, but mostly not talking at all. There was no place to sit down, but the strange man was bringing chairs from the dining room. The three of them sat down stiffly and waited, not knowing what to wait for.

An older woman got up slowly from the couch and came over to Jess's mother. Her eyes were red under her perfectly white hair. "I'm Leslie's grandmother," she said, putting out her hand.

His mother took it awkwardly. "Miz Aarons," she said in a low voice. "From up the hill."

Leslie's grandmother shook his mother's and then his father's hands. "Thank you for coming," she said. Then she turned to Jess. "You must be Jess," she said. Jess nodded. "Leslie—" Her eyes filled up with tears. "Leslie told me about you."

For a minute Jess thought she was going to say something else. He didn't want to look at her, so he gave himself over to rubbing P. T., who was hanging across his lap. "I'm sorry—" Her voice broke. "I can't bear it." The man who had opened the door came up and put his arm around her. As he was leading her out of the room, Jess could hear her crying.

He was glad she was gone. There was something weird about a woman like that crying. It was as if the lady who talked about Polident on TV had suddenly burst into tears. It didn't fit. He looked around at the room full of red-eyed adults. *Look at me*, he wanted to say to them. *I'm not crying*. A part of him stepped back and examined this thought. He was the only person his age he knew whose best friend had died. It made him important. The kids at school Monday would probably whisper around him and treat him with respect— the way they'd all treated Billy Joe Weems last year after his father had been killed in a car crash. He wouldn't have to talk to anybody if he didn't want to, and all the teachers would be especially nice to him. Momma would even make the girls be nice to him.

He had a sudden desire to see Leslie laid out. He wondered if she were back in the library or in Millsburg at one of the funeral parlors. Would they bury her in blue jeans? Or maybe that blue jumper and the flowery blouse she'd worn Easter. That would be nice. People might snicker at the blue jeans, and he didn't want anyone to snicker at Leslie when she was dead.

Bill came into the room. P. T. slid off Jess's lap and went to him. The man leaned down and rubbed the dog's back. Jess stood up.

"Jess." Bill came over to him and put his arms around him as though he had been Leslie instead of himself. Bill held him close, so that a button on his sweater was pressing painfully into Jess's forehead, but as uncomfortable as he was, Jess didn't move. He could feel Bill's body shaking, and he was afraid that if he looked up he would see Bill crying, too. He didn't want to see Bill crying. He wanted to get out of this house. It was smothering him. Why wasn't Leslie here to help him out of this? Why didn't she come running in and make everyone laugh again? *You think it's so great to die and make everyone cry and carry on. Well, it ain't.*

"She loved you, you know." He could tell from Bill's voice that he was crying. "She told me once that if it weren't for you . . ." His voice broke completely. "Thank you," he said a moment later. "Thank you for being such a wonderful friend to her."

Bill didn't sound like himself. He sounded like someone in an old mushy movie. The kind of person Leslie and Jess would laugh at and imitate later. *Boo-hooooooo, you were such a wonderful friend to her*. He couldn't help moving back, just enough to get his forehead off the stupid button. To his relief, Bill let go. He heard his father ask Bill quietly over his head about "the service."

And Bill answering quietly almost in his regular voice that they had decided to have the body cremated and were going to take the ashes to his family home in Pennsylvania tomorrow.

Cremated. Something clicked inside Jess's head. That meant Leslie was gone. Turned to ashes. He would never see her again. Not even dead. Never. How could they dare? Leslie belonged to him. More to him than anyone in the world. No one had even asked him. No one had even told him. And now he was never going to see her again, and all they could do was cry. Not for Leslie. They weren't crying for Leslie. They were crying for themselves. Just themselves. If they'd cared at all for Leslie, they would have never brought her to this rotten place. He had to hold tightly to his hands for fear he might sock Bill in the face.

He, Jess, was the only one who really cared for Leslie. But Leslie had failed him. She went and died just when he needed her the most. She went and left him. She went swinging on that rope just to show him that she was no coward. *So there, Jess Aarons*. She was probably somewhere right now laughing at him. Making fun of him like he was Mrs. Myers. She had tricked him. She had made him leave his old self behind and come into her world, and then before he was really at home in it but too late to go back, she had left him stranded there— like an astronaut wandering about on the moon. Alone.

He was never sure later just when he left the old Perkins place, but he remembered running up the hill toward his own house with angry tears streaming down his face. He banged through the door. May Belle was standing there, her brown eyes wide. "Did you see her?" she asked excitedly. "Did you see her laid out?"

He hit her. In the face. As hard as he had ever hit anything in his life. She stumbled backward from him with a little yelp. He went into the bedroom and felt under the mattress until he retrieved all his paper and the paints that Leslie had given him at Christmastime.

Ellie was standing in the bedroom door fussing at him. He pushed past her. From the couch Brenda, too, was complaining, but the only sound that really entered his head was that of May Belle whimpering.

He ran out the kitchen door and down the field all the way to the stream without looking back. The stream was a little lower than it had been when he had seen it last. Above from the crab apple tree the frayed end of the rope swung gently. *I am now the fastest runner in the fifth grade.*

He screamed something without words and flung the papers and paints into the dirty brown water. The paints floated on top, riding the current like a boat, but the papers swirled about, soaking in the muddy water, being sucked down, around, and down. He watched them all disappear. Gradually his breath quieted, and his heart slowed from its wild pace. The ground was still muddy from the rains, but he sat down anyway. There was nowhere to go. Nowhere. Ever again. He put his head down on his knee.

"That was a damn fool thing to do." His father sat down on the dirt beside him.

"I don't care. I don't care." He was crying now, crying so hard he could barely breathe.

His father pulled Jess over on his lap as though he were

Joyce Ann. "There. There," he said, patting his head. "*Shhh. Shhh.*"

"I hate her," Jess said through his sobs, "I hate her. I wish I'd never seen her in my whole life."

His father stroked his hair without speaking. Jess grew quiet. They both watched the water.

Finally his father said, "Hell, ain't it?" It was the kind of thing Jess could hear his father saying to another man. He found it strangely comforting, and it made him bold.

"Do you believe people go to hell, really go to hell, I mean?"

"You ain't worrying about Leslie Burke?"

It did seem peculiar, but still— "Well, May Belle said . . . ."

"May Belle? May Belle ain't God."

"Yeah, but how do you know what God does?"

"Lord, boy, don't be a fool. God ain't gonna send any little girls to hell."

He had never in his life thought of Leslie Burke as a little girl, but still God was sure to. She wouldn't have been eleven until November. They got up and began to walk up the hill. "I didn't mean that about hating her," he said. "I don't know what made me say that." His father nodded to show he understood.

Everyone, even Brenda, was gentle to him. Everyone except May Belle, who hung back as though afraid to have anything to do with him. He wanted to tell her he was sorry, but he couldn't. He was too tired. He couldn't just say the words. He had to make it up to her, and he was too tired to figure out how.

That afternoon Bill came up to the house. They were about to leave for Pennsylvania, and he wondered if Jess would take care of the dog until they got back.

"Sure." He was glad Bill wanted him to help. He was afraid he had hurt Bill by running away this morning. He wanted, too, to know that Bill didn't blame him for anything. But it was not the kind of question he could put into words.

He held P. T. and waved as the dusty little Italian car turned into the main road. He thought he saw them wave back, but it was too far away to be sure.

His mother had never allowed him to have a dog, but she made no objection to P. T. being in the house. P. T. jumped up on his bed, and he slept all night with P.T.'s body curled against his chest.

THIRTEEN

Building the Bridge

He woke up Saturday morning with a dull headache. It was still early, but he got up. He wanted to do the milking. His father had done it ever since Thursday night, but he wanted to go back to it, to somehow make things normal again. He shut P. T. in the shed, and the dog's whimpering reminded him of May Belle and made his headache worse. But he couldn't have P. T. yappping at Miss Bessie while he tried to milk.

No one was awake when he brought the milk in to put it away, so he poured a warm glass for himself and got a couple of pieces of light bread. He wanted his paints back, and he decided to go down and see if he could find them. He let P. T. out of the shed and gave the dog a half piece of bread.

It was a beautiful spring morning. Early wild flowers were dotting the deep green of the fields, and the sky was clean and blue. The creek had fallen well below the bank and seemed less terrifying than before. A large branch was washed up into the bank, and he hauled it up to the narrowest place and laid it bank to bank. He stepped on it, and it seemed firm, so he crossed on it, foot over foot, to the other side, grabbing the smaller branches which grew out from the main one toward the opposite bank to keep his balance. There was no sign of his paints.

He landed slightly upstream from Terabithia. If it was still Terabithia. If it could be entered across a branch instead of swung into. P. T. was left crying piteously on the other side. Then the dog took courage and paddled across the stream. The current carried him past Jess, but he made it safely to the bank and ran back, shaking great drops of cold water on Jess.

They went into the castle stronghold. It was dark and damp, but there was no evidence there to suggest that the queen had died. He felt the need to do something fitting. But Leslie was not here to tell him what it was. The anger which had possessed him yesterday flared up again. *Leslie. I'm just a dumb dodo, and you know it! What am I supposed to do?* The coldness inside of him had moved upward into his throat constricting it. He swallowed several times. It occurred to him that he probably had cancer of the throat. Wasn't that one of the seven deadly signs? *Difficulty in swallowing.* He began to sweat. He didn't want to die. Lord, he was just ten years old. He had hardly begun to live.

Leslie, were you scared? Did you know you were dying? Were you scared like me? A picture of Leslie being sucked into the cold water flashed across his brain.

"C'mon, Prince Terrien," he said quite loudly. "We must make a funeral wreath for the queen."

He sat in the clear space between the bank and the first line of trees and bent a pine bough into a circle, tying it with a piece of wet string from the castle. And because it looked cold and green, he picked spring beauties from the forest floor and wove them among the needles.

He put it down in front of him. A cardinal flew down to the bank, cocked its brilliant head, and seemed to stare at the wreath. P. T. let out a growl which sounded more like a purr. Jess put his hand on the dog to quiet him.

The bird hopped about a moment more, then flew leisurely away.

"It's a sign from the Spirits," Jess said quietly. "We made a worthy offering."

He walked slowly, as part of a great procession, though only the puppy could be seen, slowly forward carrying the queen's wreath to the sacred grove. He forced himself deep into the dark center of the grove and, kneeling, laid the wreath upon the thick carpet of golden needles.

"Father, into Thy hands I commend her spirit." He knew Leslie would have liked those words. They had the ring of the sacred grove in them.

The solemn procession wound its way through the sacred grove homeward to the castle. Like a single bird across a storm-cloud sky, a tiny peace winged its way through the chaos inside his body.

"Help! Jesse! Help me!" A scream shattered the quietness. Jess raced to the sound of May Belle's cry. She had gotten half-way across on the tree bridge and now stood there grabbing the upper branches, terrified to move either forward or backward.

"OK, May Belle." The words came out more steadily than he felt. "Just hold still. I'll get you." He was not sure the branch would hold the weight of them both. He looked down at the water. It was low enough for him to walk across, but still swift. Suppose it swept him off his feet. He decided for the branch. He inched out on it until he was close enough to touch her. He'd have to get her back to the home side of the creek. "OK," he said. "Now, back up."

"I can't!"

"I'm right here, May Belle. You think I'm gonna let you fall? Here." He put out his right hand. "Hold on to me and slide sideways on the thing."

She let go with her left hand for a moment and then grabbed the branch again.

"I'm scared, Jesse. I'm too scared."

" 'Course you're scared. Anybody'd be scared. You just gotta trust me, OK? I'm not gonna let you fall, May Belle. I promise you."

She nodded, her eyes still wide with fear, but she let go the branch and took his hand, straightening a little and swaying. He gripped her tightly.

"OK, now. It ain't far—just slide your right foot a little way, then bring your left foot up close."

"I forgot which is right."

"The front one," he said patiently. "The one closest to home."

She nodded again and obediently moved her right foot a few inches.

"Now just let go of the branch with your other hand and hold on to me tight."

She let go the branch and squeezed his hand.

"Good. You're doing great. Now slide a little ways more." She swayed but did not scream, just dug her little fingernails into the palm of his hand. "Great. Fine. You're all right." The same quiet, assuring voice of the paramedics on *Emergency*, but his heart was bongoing against his chest. "OK. OK. A little bit more, now."

When her right foot came at last to the part of the branch which rested on the bank, she fell forward, pulling him down.

"Watch it, May Belle!" He was off balance, but he fell, not into the stream, but with his chest across May Belle's legs, his

own legs waving in the empty air above the water. "Whew!" He was laughing with relief. "Whatcha trying to do, girl, kill me?"

She shook her head a solemn no, "I know I swore on the Bible not to follow you, but I woke up this morning and you was gone."

"I had to do some things."

She was scraping at the mud on her bare legs. "I just wanted to find you, so you wouldn't be so lonesome." She hung her head. "But I got too scared."

He pulled himself around until he was sitting beside her. They watched P. T. swimming across, the current carrying him too swiftly, but he not seeming to mind. He climbed out well below the crab apple and came running back to where they sat.

"Everybody gets scared sometimes, May Belle. You don't have to be ashamed." He saw a flash of Leslie's eyes as she was going in to the girls' room to see Janice Avery. "Everybody gets scared."

"P. T. ain't scared, and he even saw Leslie . . ."

"It ain't the same for dogs. It's like the smarter you are, the more things can scare you."

She looked at him in disbelief. "But you weren't scared."

"Lord, May Belle, I was shaking like Jello."

"You're just saying that."

He laughed. He couldn't help being glad she didn't believe him. He jumped up and pulled her to her feet. "Let's go eat." He let her beat him to the house.

When he walked into the basement classroom, he saw Mrs. Myers had already had Leslie's desk taken out of the front of the room. Of course, by Monday Jess knew; but still, but still, at the bus stop he looked up, half expecting to see her running up across the field, her lovely, even, rhythmic run. Maybe she was already at school—Bill had dropped her off, as he did some days when she was late for the bus—but then when Jess came into the room, her desk was no longer there. Why were they all in such a rush to be rid of her? He put his head down on his own desk, his whole body heavy and cold.

He could hear the sounds of the whispers but not the words. Not that he wanted to hear the words. He was suddenly ashamed that he'd thought he might be regarded with respect by the other kids. Trying to profit for himself from Leslie's death. *I wanted to be the best—the fastest runner in the school —and now I am*. Lord, he made himself sick. He didn't care what the others said or what they thought, just as long as they left him alone—just so long as he didn't have to talk to them or meet their stares. They had all hated Leslie. Except maybe Janice. Even after they'd given up trying to make Leslie miserable, they'd kept on despising her—as though there was one of them worth the nail on Leslie's little toe. And even he himself had entertained the traitorous thought that now he would be the fastest.

Mrs. Myers barked the command to stand for the allegiance. He didn't move. Whether he couldn't or wouldn't, he didn't really care. What could she do to him, after all?

"Jesse Aarons. Will you step out into the hall. Please."

He raised his leaden body and stumbled out of the room. He thought he heard Gary Fulcher giggle, but he couldn't be sure. He leaned against the wall and waited for Monster Mouth Myers to finish singing "O Say Can You See?" and join him. He could hear her giving the class some sort of assignment in ᴇtic before she came out and quietly closed the door her.

OK. Shoot. I don't care.

She came over so close to him that he could smell her dime-store powder.

"Jesse." Her voice was softer than he had ever heard it, but he didn't answer. Let her yell. He was used to that.

"Jesse," she repeated. "I just want to give you my sincere sympathy." The words were like a Hallmark card, but the tone was new to him.

He looked up into her face, despite himself. Behind her turned-up glasses, Mrs. Myers' narrow eyes were full of tears. For a minute he thought he might cry himself. He and Mrs. Myers standing in the basement hallway, crying over Leslie Burke. It was so weird he almost laughed instead.

"When my husband died"—Jess could hardly imagine Mrs. Myers ever having had a husband—"people kept telling me not to cry, kept trying to make me forget." Mrs. Myers loving, mourning. How could you picture it? "But I didn't want to forget." She took her handkerchief from her sleeve and blew her nose. "Excuse me," she said. "This morning when I came in, someone had already taken out her desk." She stopped and blew her nose again. "It—it—we—I never had such a student. In all my years of teaching. I shall always be grateful—"

He wanted to comfort her. He wanted to unsay all the things he had said about her—even unsay the things Leslie had said. Lord, don't let her ever find out.

"So—I realize. If it's hard for me, how much harder it must be for you. Let's try to help each other, shall we?"

"Yes'm." He couldn't think of anything else to say. Maybe some day when he was grown, he would write her a letter and tell her that Leslie Burke had thought she was a great teacher or something. Leslie wouldn't mind. Sometimes like the Barbie doll you need to give people something that's for them, not just something that makes you feel good giving it. Because

Mrs. Myers had helped him already by understanding that he would never forget Leslie.

He thought about it all day, how before Leslie came, he had been a nothing—a stupid, weird little kid who drew funny pictures and chased around a cow field trying to act big—trying to hide a whole mob of foolish little fears running riot inside his gut.

It was Leslie who had taken him from the cow pasture into Terabithia and turned him into a king. He had thought that was it. Wasn't king the best you could be? Now it occurred to him that perhaps Terabithia was like a castle where you came to be knighted. After you stayed for a while and grew strong you had to move on. For hadn't Leslie, even in Terabithia, tried to push back the walls of his mind and make him see beyond to the shining world—huge and terrible and beautiful and very fragile? (Handle with care—everything—even the predators.)

Now it was time for him to move out. She wasn't there, so he must go for both of them. It was up to him to pay back to the world in beauty and caring what Leslie had loaned him in vision and strength.

As for the terrors ahead—for he did not fool himself that they were all behind him—well, you just have to stand up to your fear and not let it squeeze you white. Right, Leslie?

Right.

🌿

Bill and Judy came back from Pennsylvania on Wednesday with a U-Haul truck. No one ever stayed long in the old Perkins place. "We came to the country for her sake. Now that she's gone . . ." They gave Jesse all of Leslie's books and her paint set with three pads of real watercolor paper. "She would want you to have them," Bill said.

Jess and his dad helped them load the U-Haul, and noon-time his mother brought down ham sandwiches and coffee, a little scared the Burkes wouldn't want to eat her food, but needing, Jess knew, to do something. At last the truck was filled, and the Aaronses and the Burkes stood around awk-wardly, no one knowing how to say good-bye.

"Well," Bill said. "If there's anything we've left that you want, please help yourself."

"Could I have some of the lumber on the back porch?" Jess asked.

"Yes, of course. Anything you see." Bill hesitated, then continued. "I meant to give you P. T.," he said. "But"—he looked at Jess and his eyes were those of a pleading little boy —"but I can't seem to give him up."

"It's OK. Leslie would want you to keep him."

The next day after school, Jess went down and got the lumber he needed, carrying it a couple of boards at a time to the creek bank. He put the two longest pieces across at the narrow place upstream from the crab apple tree, and when he was sure they were as firm and even as he could make them, he began to nail on the crosspieces.

"Whatcha doing, Jess?" May Belle had followed him down again as he had guessed she might.

"It's a secret, May Belle."

"Tell me."

"When I finish, OK?"

"I swear on the Bible I won't tell nobody. Not Billy Jean, not Joyce Ann, not Momma—" She was jerking her head back and forth in solemn emphasis.

"Oh, I don't know about Joyce Ann. You might want to tell Joyce Ann sometime."

"Tell Joyce Ann something that's a secret between you and me?" The idea seemed to horrify her.

"Yeah, I was just thinking about it."

Her face sagged. "Joyce Ann ain't nothing but a baby."

"Well, she wouldn't likely be a queen first off. You'd have to train her and stuff."

"Queen? Who gets to be queen?"

"I'll explain it when I finish, OK?"

And when he finished, he put flowers in her hair and led her across the bridge—the great bridge into Terabithia—which might look to someone with no magic in him like a few planks across a nearly dry gully.

"*Shhh*," he said. "Look."

"Where?"

"Can't you see 'um?" he whispered. "All the Terabithians standing on tiptoe to see you."

"*Me?*"

"*Shhh*, yes. There's a rumor going around that the beautiful girl arriving today might be the queen they've been waiting for."